Snarky a

John Stamp

Illustrated by Paul Taylor-Smith

For information contact :
stampjohn@me.com
johnstampmusic.com

Written for Aubin my Grandson during the spring of 2020.

A time when we looked at each other through screens, waved at windows and stood six feet apart.

Sometimes it all felt strange, other times we started to understand the new normal. You can't squash love – it has a way of travelling, whether through a window, a smile, a hug, a screen or across thousands of miles.

Huge credit to Paul Taylor-Smith for his herculean efforts and weekly updates from Texas to Derbyshire.

Amanda – finally did it!!

Contents

CHAPTER ONE
152 and counting

Sitting in her garden, letting the early spring sun of late March 2020 wash over her face, Alice was the picture of an elderly woman at peace with the world. Deep inside that brain, under the slightly battered baseball cap, lay a mind that plotted and schemed. Thoughts darted around like scampering monkeys chattering to each other. Alice was a master at herding them together and making them hatch a plan. A plan that would benefit Alice and maybe no one else.

Alan looked out of the window. He'd been peering out of his window for about ten minutes and there was a huge amount of nothing going on. He turned back to look at his bed, still unmade with bits of Lego on the floor. One sinister piece looking very guilty and sharp just a few yards from the bed. He'd stood on that last night as he got up to go for a wee, which annoyingly his dad called a tiddle! It didn't annoy him as much as the sharp pain that still shot through his foot.

Lego, you save up, you buy it, you scratch your head, you read again and again, you build it…then you stand on it at 3am and shout made up swear words.

"Ooooooooooh squiddle fips and flupper ships!!!" Made up swear words were a Godsend to Alan. Being grounded would have been a daily happening at 43 Haddon Street if he hadn't thought of it.

Alan stayed looking out of the window for a few more minutes, hoping to catch a glimpse of Mrs Snark. His mum said she'd spotted Mrs Snark putting the bins out yesterday morning.

"Good things come to those who wait," thought Alan; "I'll count to 153 again."

He had a superstition that the number 153 was the perfect point when things would happen. Testing it out many times, waiting for his mate Jakub to come round, he'd count to 153 and almost 9 times out of 10 Jakub would appear as he reached 153. Well maybe 7 or 5 times out of ten. Hard to remember numbers isn't it.

He tried again......147, 148,

149,

150,

151, 152 – Mrs Snark appeared at the front door and peered out, pulled her tongue out at the sky and then disappeared behind the door again.

Alan jumped back – "what the jiggery packet of pink peaches?"

"Pulling your tongue at the sky…who does that?"

Alan had a bad feeling about Mrs Snark. In the same way you do about a villain in a movie. They just have an air of no good about them. Maybe a kind of turned up side to their mouth, or mysterious looking hair, or a cape that trails behind them as they walk. Mrs Snark had none of these… she just looked dodgy.

Her strange dress sense was a small annoyance, her sneaky eyes as she took the bins out, shady. Just the loudness of how snappily she shut the front door behind her gave you a hint that maybe all was not good.

Alan Sheen lives at 43 Haddon Street, Lower Bolsever, Derbyshire. He's 10 and has one tooth that stills wobbles. His dad Eric is a postman; mum Jane looks after Alan's Grandma Moira who lives two miles away. He and his family have lived in Lower Bolsever for seven years, before then they lived in Chesterfield, which is also in Derbyshire. Alan can't remember any of that time of his life.

Just a week ago, when the world had felt like a different place, Alan would ride his bike in the lanes around his house. He'd go to school, play with Jakub in the park and sometimes go fishing with his dad. Last Tuesday the Prime Minister said

"We've got to stay indoors, because Coronavirus is very nasty and makes your eyes and nose runny, makes your trousers fall down, old peoples hair falls out, some strange people do dances that look like chickens and ......and errrrrm various other stuff that I can't mention."

At least that's what Alan wished he'd have said. The Prime Minister had said lots of other words and basically scared the 'flying piddly poos' out of most people. Alan's Dad just said – "Well no more going outside, we'll have to stay in."

The funny thing is, when someone tells you to stay in, all you wanna do is go out and when someone says 'go out' all you wanna do is stay in.

The first two days were ok. Alan read some books by famous people who also judged TV talent shows. Which is the law for all children under the age of eleven. Watched some TV, his mum planned some home school stuff. Dad Eric went to work as usual as he was a postman and everybody still needed post.

The evening of day two, Alan lay in bed and his mind started to wander. When would all this get back to normal? When would the Prime Minister stop telling us about the dangers of sneezing on people, when would it be ok to pick your nose again, scratch your bum, stand close to your friend Jakub.... maybe it'd be a whole 153 days. "Jiggery blue pigs." thought Alan, as he scratched his bum.

The good news was that Jakubs house was just over the road...they could literally see each other. So the next morning Alan drew a sign on some big pieces of paper.

"HEY JAKUB, ITS ME ALAN, ARE YOU OK?"

Alan put the paper in his bedroom window with Sellotape. Then he thought, "What a funny word Sellotape is! Why not sticky tape?"

CHAPTER TWO

Hair of the Pyggs

You're probably wondering who Mrs Snark is? No? Ok I'll come back to her later. Alice Snark takes a lot of explaining, but as you're not wondering about her I'll tell you about Mr Pygg who lives next door. Well he lives with his sister Ms Pygg, The Pyggs. I know it's a funny name but they're so not like Pigs at all, very clean and tidy people with a very shaky three-wheel car that almost tips over as it goes around the corner. They're about 147 years old (combined) and between them have about 150,000 hairs on their heads, mostly a nice grey. (The average human has 100,00 hairs). The majority of the hairs are Lottie Pygg's.

To add to the sense of mystery Ron dresses like a French spy. He has such a lovely dapper way of wearing his beret and cravat. Looks a little out of place on Haddon Street, but Ron was happy.

I suppose this all added to Alan's imagination. Spies and criminals lurk on every corner – well in the corners of Alan's mind. Lottie in the Russian hat and Ron with the French beret…. who would suspect anything!!

When Alan's playing football in the garden Ms Pygg sometimes spies through the fence and shouts 'GOAL' as if she's trying to join in. This makes Alan feel a little weird, as she never says anything else, just shouts "GOAL."

The Pygg's and Mrs Snark live directly opposite each other on Haddon Street. Jakub lives next door to Mrs Snark. (You still with me here? Don't fall asleep.)

The Pyggs and Mrs Snark catch the bus into Derby together every Monday morning. Well they used to before they were afraid of trousers falling down, people coughing on them and the last of the Pyggs five hairs falling out.

Now they stay in and a man in a white van brings them some food. The man leaves everything on the doorstep. Rings the bell and drives off. The Pyggs and Mrs Snark cautiously open their doors, look around then reach out and pull the food and the parcels in.

Across the UK and most of the world, people were becoming afraid. Oh they knew about the Common Cold and Flu and maybe even Ebola. They knew people could die and many did. In fact thousands of mainly older people died of viruses and colds each year. But this virus, this new one, had come so suddenly and well…the Prime Minister Boris Johnson had looked very serious and nervous when he came on telly and told everyone to stay home. Many people made themselves feel a bit happier by making up a few stories,

"Its from China and its their fault, it'll go away in a few weeks, the scientists will come up with an answer very soon, just you wait and see."

Living on Haddon Street there were about ninety older people, you know those over the age of about 70 or 75. Some were aged 80 and maybe 90. They would need to rely on help from all kinds of people. They would need to trust that the country and the Government would find an answer. A bit like their mums and dads did back in the war years. Over the coming weeks many heroes would appear. Some dressed as doctors and nurses and care workers, but many just in their jeans and T-shirts. Heroes who didn't wear masks or tights or have lasers., or big S's on their shirts. Everyday people doing amazing stuff.

About a month ago, before all this lockdown, Alan's mum had been visiting his grandma Moira. Granny Moira is almost 83 and a bit. Granny Moira used to be a swimming teacher; in fact she was an epic swimmer and had swum across lake Windermere. Which Alan hadn't heard of but his mum said it's like swimming to Tesco and back. Which meant nothing to Alan but sounded very hard, as there was no water between Haddon Street and Tesco. Grandma Moira had very bad eyesight and had the best glasses Alan had ever seen; very thick, a bit tinted but so strong that she could see Alan's face. Because she could see Alan's face she loved to stroke it, under his chin which annoyed Alan but he couldn't tell her because she was old. He didn't say any of his made up swear words in front of

Grandma Moira – she would know – she was very switched on – as he'd heard his mum say. "Jiggery Pimple sniffers." Alan thought.

Alan's mum came back after visiting Grandma and sat in her chair and shook her head. She started to giggle and couldn't tell Alan what she was laughing at cos the words wouldn't come out. You know how annoying it is when someone has a joke and they can't tell you cos they're laughing, and laughing and laughing. Alan counted to 153. She was still shaking her shoulders. After a while Alan's mum Jane took a breath. "Alan," she said, "Grandma is so wonderful, but sometimes her eyes mean she does the funniest things." Alan waited… "I took Grandma to the cinema this afternoon to watch a film she'd heard about. We got in ok; I guided her along to the seat. As we went to sit down Grandma took off her coat and thinking she was hanging it on the seat in front she draped it over the man's head who was sitting there. The man was so surprised he stayed sitting with the coat over his head for quite a while before I noticed and took it off him." "Oh Grandma!" Alan thought, wishing he'd seen it himself. Alan's Grandma was someone whom he could always get a straight answer from, when grownups weren't telling you the full story… she would be a great help to him in the weeks ahead.

CHAPTER THREE

Staying in

"If you imagine that the world outside is kind of all doing ok, then staying in is just another version of going out. Except you're inside." Alan knew what he meant; just when he tried to explain it to his mum and dad it all came out wrong. Alan had popped into the lounge to cheer his mum and dad up with his newfound wisdom, just as they were watching the news. The BBC had become a little bored of our own UK leader Boris Johnson telling us how he planned to get through this pandemic and had decided to show some CNN American News. Donald Trump was stood behind his lectern, a preacher style desk thing with two big flags waving behind his head. The breeze was starting to blow his hair around a little. Alan could see in Trump's eyes that he was aware that seven zillion people around the world were also aware that he was aware that his hair was lifting up from the left side. The wind picked up a little more and the thick cotton wool texture of his hair, orange and faded light brown started to really lift like a teapot lid. He raised his hand and patted it down. Alan said to his dad "Dad do you think that Donald Trump – trumps?" "Of course he does Alan, otherwise he'd be full of hot air." Alan looked at his dad "That is the funniest thing I've heard in squillions of years." He didn't know it but his dad had just made Alan's day.

Donald Trump began his speech.

"Fellow Americans, this is a wartime unprecedented time of our lives and I am the man to save you all. Don't worry too much about this little bug, it's just like a cold and by Easter we'll all be having a beautiful old time and dancing in the streets. My team who are the most amazing in the world, and universe are working very very very hard to bring you a solution and to make me look good. Some people are gonna die with this disease who haven't died before. This is very sad. I'm the president of the greatest nation in the world and I am your leader, you are my followers and everything's gonna be good. Today I spoke with the leader of China and we said 'Hi', after that we needed an interpreter and I can't remember much else about what we said…but don't worry things are gonna get better."

Alan wondered how many people would feel a little scared after that speech. But then he remembered what his Grandma Moira had said… "Alan, just do what Mr Boris Johnson said and wash your hands and stay indoors and concentrate on all the good things that you can do…like your homework for starters."

The BBC cut back to a reporter outside Buckingham Palace. "The Queen has been seen walking her dogs around the grounds of the palace today."

"She also had no visitors and is isolating with Prince Phillip." Alan wondered if they had a problem with getting toilet rolls for the 200 toilets they have at the palace and if her servants were allowed to pass each other on the staircases.

The Government had said that people could spend one hour a day outside. Getting some exercise they say is very good for your mind and body. Alan liked to ride his bike down Haddon Street or play football in his garden. The garden was about fifty feet long by thirty feet wide. At almost exactly 4.5 feet tall, 54 inches or 1.3 metres Alan stood as tall as the average boy in England. His small round and chubby face had a very open and friendly look. When people met Alan they knew he was ok, he had a smile that said 'its ok to like me'. Not that everyone did like him, some not so nice kids at school sometimes were rude and said nasty things, but Alan had a way of shrugging it off. Playing football was a big part of the school day at St Peter's School. The boys and one or two girls, who generally had more skill than the boys, would play in the small playground. Full sized footballs were banned but a tennis ball or some-times a rolled up sock would be used. Alan didn't always get chosen to play in these lunchtime war zone games, where shoes get scuffed and jumpers were pulled and tugged and school bags made up the goal posts.

But at home, Alan chose the team.

He imagined himself as part of a big team and ran madly around the garden.

"...and Sheen has the ball, passes it to himself, then back to Sheen, he's gone straight past two roses....oh my Lord look out he's on a roll..... Sheen tackled Sheen and its gone straight back to Sheen.......can he get past the other Sheen.....he's bounced it off the wall and Sheens got it again...he's now sprinting past the washing line....its a ....."

From behind the fence came a weak little voice "GOAL."

Alan turned sharply, his breath heavy from running. In the gap of the fence he could see Ms Pyggs eyes looking at him ..."GOAL" much louder this time.

CHAPTER FOUR

Yoga rolls

Alan dived on the floor and lay still. He could hear Ms Pygg's breathing from behind the fence. He lay still for what seemed like an age, staring at the sky. As he lay there he could see the house on the other side of his. The house where Tom Rhodes lived.

Tom was an exercise freak and muscle builder, boxer, weight lifter, yoga master, snooker champion and ran the corner shop called 'Toms Tins and stuff'.

In the window, that would be Tom's bedroom, he could see the shadow of Tom doing some yoga. He seemed to be bending himself in half and the shadow looked like he was balancing a snake on his nose whilst juggling a watering can. "Holy Mother of Elvis." thought Alan…his new favourite saying. He realised that while he'd been trying to work out what Tom was doing he'd forgotten about Ms Pygg. He couldn't hear her breathing now. All quiet.

At that moment the backdoor of the Pygg's house opened and out came Mr Pygg.

"Hey Lottie what are you doing looking at the fence?" said Ron. "Well I was watching Alan play football, but he seems to have gone in now."

"…we haven't time to be doing that Lottie… we're almost out of toilet rolls, we need to get some more."

Lottie Pygg huffed; Alan could hear her wipe her nose with what he assumed was her hanky or sleeve. "Well, we'll do an online shop Ron, I'm sure Tesco will have some."

"Tried that Lottie, and Aldi and Morrisons and Sainsbury's. All gone…. not a sheet between them."

He heard Ms Pygg grunt a little and shuffle her feet back and two. "Why don't we ask Alice to help us Ron?" "She said she'd help with anything we need. Alice Snark said she had the way to find lots of things. Surely toilet rolls cant be that hard to find." Ron puffed his chest out "Lottie this is wartime England…we're in a battle for survival here and you've got to do your bit. We can't expect Alice Snark to bail us out…. Come on, let's slice some newspaper into small squares and hang them on a nail next to the loo. That's what we used to do as a kid. We had a loo at the end of the garden – you remember, our old dad used to make sure there was always newspaper hanging on the nail."

"Yeah I remember Ron, I'm sure I had The Daily Mirror stories all over my bum." Ron chuckled as he turned on his heels and headed back to the house.

Alan lay still for a while. He could hear his breathing get a little louder. The shadow of Tom was now of him lifting weights – he could hear him straining…"One and Two and Three."

It had been 24 hours since Alan had put the note to Jakub in the window. When he walked into his bedroom Alan could see a faint outline of some small pieces of white paper in Jakub's bedroom. In fact so small that you'd need to be two feet away to read them. "What the flabber chuckle sweet pickle is Jakub thinking I am?" thought Alan, "A human telescope?? "

Good job he knew where his dad kept the binoculars. Hanging behind the door of the garage. Alan grabbed them and ran back to the bedroom and strained his eyes to see. HI ALAN, IM OK, BUT MY MUMS CHIPPED A TOOTH!

Alan put his hands on his head and thought, "This is going to be a long conversation."

As Alan lay on his bed that night he thought back to the garden that afternoon. Ms Pygg had been acting very weird and he felt a bit weird-ed-out that she and Mr Pygg…Ron as she called him, were talking about Mrs Snark being able to get lots of things. Almost like Mrs Snark knew things that other people didn't.

A few days ago Alan's dad Eric had popped over to Mrs Snark's house to drop a letter that had mistakenly been delivered to their address.

When he got back he told Alans mum Jane about something he'd over heard her saying from behind the door. It sounded like she was on the telephone Eric said. She was almost shouting and saying…"Just get the rolls Gary, get the damn rolls." Alan sat with his head in a book as he overheard this.

"Rolls of what, sausage rolls, egg rolls. Aha – maybe code for Rolls Royce. They were smugglers of expensive cars. What crazy sniffle wiffle person is buying cars these days." he thought. This was testing his brain and getting to sleep was going to be very difficult. Alan lay thinking again. Asking Gary for rolls of something, an angry Mrs Snark. What was in the white boxes that arrived from the white vans that dropped the food off? He was going to need Jakub's help in all this. But they couldn't communicate with little posted pieces of paper on the window cos the crooked neighbour would see it. What could he do? Then it came to him.

CHAPTER FIVE

Some things aren't what they appear

145,146, 147, 148…

Come on, come on, come on 149

Dad come on…

150, 151, 152, 153…arrrrrrggghhh.

"Squirting flying monkey baskets!"

Alan jumped from one foot to the other, outside the bathroom door.

"Dad I am literally going to wee all over the floor out here, come on!!"

The Sheen house was a 1930's semi-detached with one bathroom. Alan and his mum and dad usually managed very well. But today the stars had not aligned, the cars had crashed, the train had come off the tracks and all that Alan could finally shout through the door was….

"Good job I don't need a poo or you'd really be sorry!"

Eric stood looking in the mirror. He could hear the commotion outside the bathroom. He could tell that Alan was close to the edge. "Right – I'm going out to wee in the garden and whoever sees me, sees me!!!"

Eric took a deep breath and came back to the moment. He'd been thinking about the last few days. Travelling around the lanes and highways of Derbyshire, delivering much needed post to the lonely, the old, the scared, some people unaware of how crazy all this was. The Prime Minister had called it a national crisis. Eric felt fortunate that he was in a job that he could still do and also that he was helping people. He was now about to start an afternoon shift and as he got ready and shaved, it all became very real. Eric took one more breath and remembered what his old dad used to say 'this too will pass Eric, all things will pass'. To be fair his dad wasn't talking about a massive world-changing event like the Coronavirus, he usually meant the weather, or some homework that Eric had forgotten to do. But …it made sense. "This too will pass."

As Eric strode out of the bathroom, Alan virtually crawled between his legs and quickly locked the door. He was relieved that he hadn't gone for a wee in the garden as he had an awful vision of Ms Pygg, Lottie shouting 'goal ' as he took a tiddle.

Back in his bedroom Alan looked across the street and could still see small pieces of paper in Jakubs window. His idea of how to speak with Jakub, about all manner of things, not least the mysterious bad feeling he had, still hung in his mind.

In the corner of his eye he glimpsed Mrs Snark as she stepped out of her front door. She was wearing her full length green …well no way to describe it other than a shooting jacket…like something you'd wear if you were going to hunt rabbits and pigeons in the fields. On her head was a grey baseball cap with 'Scarborough's got talent' written on the front. She had a hospital grade plastic PPE mask on her face and blue surgical gloves. And on her feet? Well she was sporting her pink slippers. She stood facing the Pygg's house. Arching her neck as if trying to get their attention. She walked to the edge of the pavement and stood still. Alan crouched down and crawled to the window. He popped his head just high enough over the windowsill that he could see her, but Mrs Snark couldn't see him. The windows in his house were so well made that you couldn't really hear much outside. There was usually traffic going by. But this past week or so, barely a car or van, or bus went by. The quiet was eerie. Alan's eyes darted between the paper note in Jakub's window and Mrs Snark's alien looking outfit standing in the street. What did Jakub write? What was Mrs Snark doing, how could he tell what she was saying to the Pyggs?

Mrs Snark smiled across the road. The large plastic mask almost magnifies her grouchy looking features. Lottie Pygg stepped forward. He could only see the back of Lotties head as she was facing away from him. But he could see Mrs Snarks mouth moving as she spoke across the road. Her hands were moving and she was describing something, showing how big it should be. Alan was transfixed.

Jakub appeared at his window and from his viewpoint he could see the top of Alan's head as he crouched behind the window.

Jakub hadn't scanned the street below him and hadn't spotted the scenario that played out. He couldn't see the reason why Alan might be peeping over the sill. Jakub began to wave at Alan and opened the window to shout. As he did he looked down to the street.

In one swift moment, with his head out of the window Jakubs words moved from

"Alllllllaaaaann"

to

"Helloooooo Ladiiieees and a good morning to youoooo."

He closed the window and fell to his bed.

Mrs Snark and Lottie snapped their heads around and stared bewildered at Jakubs bedroom. "What a strange boy," wheezed Mrs Snark. "strange times and strange boy."

CHAPTER SIX
Football murderer

Not the oldest, but the person who'd lived the longest on Haddon Street is Alice Snark. Almost a good solid twenty years. Well exactly twenty years to be honest. Not that long really, other streets had people who'd been born there and still lived there. Some for over fifty years.

January 23rd 2000 she'd carried her cat Jinxy across the doorway and breathed in the stale air. The house had been empty for eighteen months; a cold chill blew through as she closed the door behind her. Jinxy the cat had lived for just a few months after arriving. Alice had a 'boyfriend' live with her for many years; Alan had heard his mum say. But these past few years she'd been alone. There was some mystery about the 'boyfriend' too. He seems to have been seen carrying a small paper bag out of the house one June morning – never to be seen again. It seemed a bit strange to Alan hearing Mrs Snark's friend being called a 'boyfriend' – he looked quite old from what Alan had seen. He was no more a boy than Mrs Snark was a ballerina or a Scuba diver!!

Jakub lived right next door to Mrs Snark. He had some stories that he amused Alan with. The most alarming being how she started to burst Jakub's footballs if they went over her garden. Jakub went around the first time and asked for his ball back. She came to the door with a growly face and said "Keep the ball over your side of the fence sonny or it'll be feeling a little deflated." She cackled and laughed to herself as she shut the door. Jakub tried so hard to keep the ball over his side but just a few days later, whilst tackling himself and trying to win the 'Inside of Jakubs head world cup 2018' he took a flying shot at goal. The ball hit the post, the fence post, then bounced back with amazing force and slapped Jakub in the face… stinging his cheek. Jakub fell back and with an open mouth watched the ball, in slow motion as it arched over the fence and thudded into Mrs Snark's garden.

As Jakub recovered from the slap of the ball he heard a door click. Footsteps swished up the garden path, all happening just over the fence. He winced as he heard a sharp stabbing sound…. followed by a swoosh of air as it escaped from the ball. Jakub felt like he'd witnessed a murder. The execution of his favourite football. "Nobody, ….yes nobody messes with the roses and beautiful flora and fauna that is my garden…you stupid boy."

The dramatic words echoed over Jakub's fence and around the garden. The door slammed.

Bringing his thoughts back to the scene on the street, Alan peeked over the windowsill again, and watched as Mrs Snark turned and headed back into her house. Ms Pygg turned and looked straight up at Alan's window. She smiled and waved at Alan…. he dropped to the floor so hard he banged his chin. "Grappling chuffer farts," he muttered to himself, "she knew I was there."

Now was the time to work together with Jakub. Jakub knew how this woman operated. He'd lost seven very fine and healthy footballs to the random temper of Mrs Snark. Jakub would know what to do.

Heading down stairs and into the garage Alan had a plan. Mum was over at Grandma Moiras, probably stood outside the window keeping her six feet apart. Dad was on his afternoon shift, probably leaving boxes outside the houses of people who were sat glued to the news. It occurred to Alan that we were all living as if the country had a bad case of bad breath. No one wanted to get too close. How were we going to greet each other in a few months' time, will people still bump elbows or stand six feet apart and shout "How's it going?" Maybe masks will become the new hat; you take your mask off the coat stand as you leave the house. Will he be able to ever hug Grandma? Will she be able to come for tea? Grandma was one of the people at high risk of being very poorly with this sickness and many people were dying.

Alan stood in the garage and looked at his dad's fishing gear. It leant against the wall in the corner. He and his dad quite often, well, some weekends would go over to Ackers Pit, a small quarry just outside of

Lower Bolsever. They would spend the morning catching Perch and Tench. Gently unhook the fish and throw them back. Alan had learnt to use the catapult to fire some bait into the water and most of all, he had learnt to wait. Maybe that's where he got the saying from…'Good things come to those who wait'.

Alan walked over to the fishing gear and opened dad's tackle box.

The catapult lay at the top. It shined. The whole thing was made of cast iron. About thirty years old, with a wooden handle shaped over the iron. The wooden handle beautifully worn from the many fishing trips, polished and brown. The elastic hung limp and ready to be pulled back in action, the little pouch where the bait and stones would go was also very well worn. Alan loved this catapult.

Back in his bedroom Alan gathered some of the pieces of his Lego that lay on the floor. Right he thought… "Just get Jakubs attention, fire some words over to him…. then we can do some investigation."

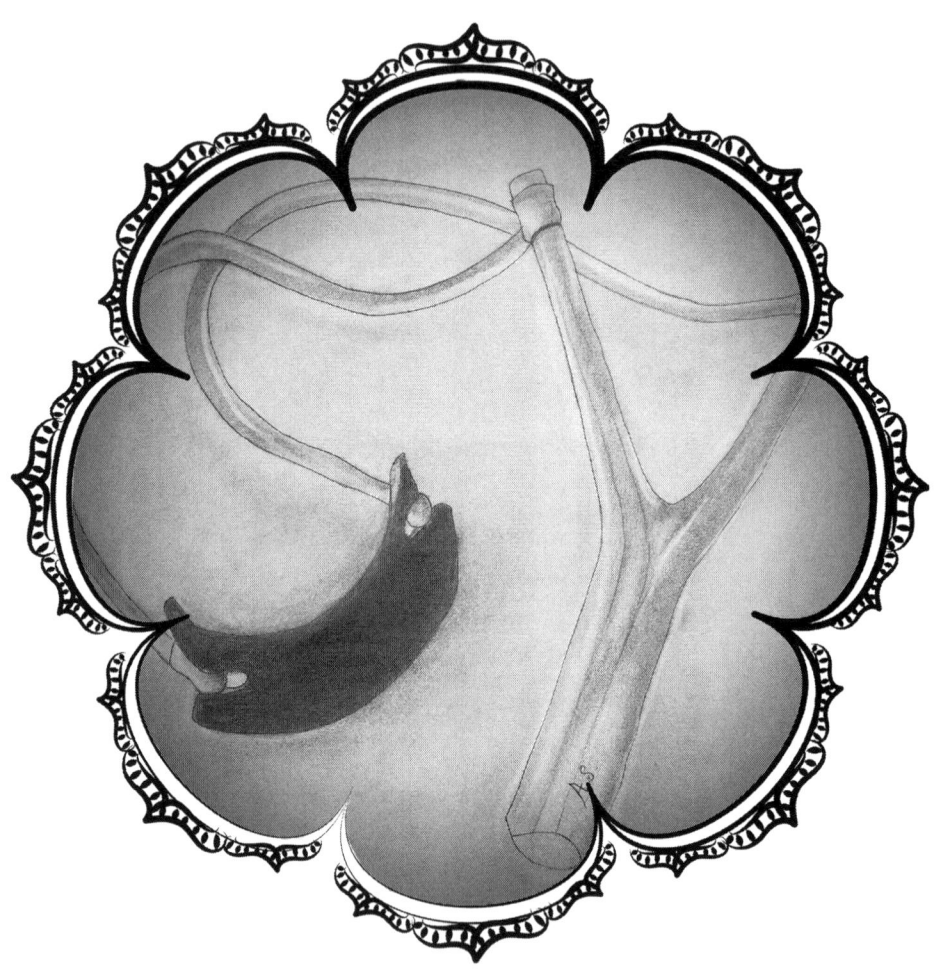

CHAPTER SEVEN

Why wait when you can do?

Things were similar in the Second World War or WW2 as Alan's Grand-dad Nigel used to call it. Granddad Nigel had died when Alan was just six, but Alan remembered him. He used to do magic tricks that weren't really magic tricks. They were more like older people thinking they could outsmart small children and fool them, or so Alan thought. Everybody knows kids just play along to make adults feel good.

He would hide a coin in his hand and then put his hand behind Alan's head and pull it quickly out of his ear. Alan worked this out after about a week but kept playing along, as he didn't want to spoil the fun for Granddad Nigel. He also used to put his thumbs together and make it look as if he was pulling his thumb in half…seemed a little strange to Alan that your Granddad would want to pull his thumb in half right in front of his Grandson's face… "Good job I worked it out, I'd be scream-ing the place down if not!"

This time was similar to the war because of the following reasons thought Alan:

- We all had one common enemy; (most of the world haven't seen the Covid19 enemy, apart from scientists with their magnifying equipment.) In the war people took the government's word for it that there was an enemy because bombs fell out of the sky and many people were killed.

- Everything feels very different and all the adults and some kids are watching the news all the time and waiting to hear what the enemy has done.

- The country has a big plan of how we're going to beat this enemy.

- The country is spending lots of money on building weapons to defeat the enemy. Finding the big bomb of a vaccine to smash this thing was very important.
- People need to get their brains together and find a solution.
- Mum and dad are being extra kind to me and maybe that's how it was in the war.
- Children aren't allowed to play on the streets in-case the enemy gets them…drops the very tiny or big bomb.
- The Prime Minister is slightly crazy with a wild look in his eye… but you know what, he's probably the man to get us outta this mess!! Winston Churchill was a great wartime leader; Granddad Nigel had mentioned him a few times.

Alan loaded the catapult with the Lego and opened the window.

You're probably wondering why Alan and Jakub didn't just use Smart Phones and call each other? Or text or maybe Whatsapp, Snapchat, facebook messenger, Instagram….and a whole range of other fabulous cyber communication methods? Well, just over twelve months ago both Jakub and Alan's parents had made a promise that the boys could have phones when they reached the age of ten. The excitement of this news had been huge in their lives. "Imagine, we can call each other, facetime, play online chess." The list went on.

In true catastrophic fashion, in the same way a restaurant owner may have felt as the world caved in when he planned to open his new diner on the 23rd March 2020 – only to be told "WE'RE LOCKING DOWN!" A huge wave of online bullying happened at Alan and Jakub's school St Joseph's. At almost the same moment on the same street with the same groaning sound coming from two almost ten-year-old boys as the news was announced "We're saying no to a mobile phone for another year." Announced Alan and Jakubs parents. "We really don't want you to be involved in some of the nasty things that have been happening." Some children had said very bad things about other children and shared it with lots of others, making people feel very upset. Some children had said they were looking forward to Alan and Jakub having a phone so they could do the same to them. The head teacher had heard about this and all sorts of meetings had happened.

The sad fact was that what should have been a great thing to have, a mobile phone, was in-fact something that was now being used as a weapon.

It just takes a few bad eggs to spoil things, and what they did stank. Both Eric and Jane and Sally and Keith (Jakub's parents) had met with the head teacher. The Bullies had been dealt with and lessons had been learned, but both sets of parents had come to an agreement – "You know what, ten is too young to have a mobile phone. We'll review it in a year." Alan remembered feeling relieved when the idea of a phone went away. He played more football, wrote some funny poems, rode his bike and basically had a better time. Although when it happened he did say, "Big fat fluffer puddles."

The pieces of Lego whizzed through the air. Arched up over the road and landed about ten feet from Jakub's window. Alan tried for the second time. The third time Alan changed the missile and the leg off a small Lego soldier twanged on Jakub's window. Jakub was cutting out some pictures from football magazines and glueing them to a sheet of paper to make a poster for his room. Twang went the window – Jakub sat upright and looked around the room. Nothing …he carried on glueing. Twang again. It took about ten pieces of Lego and four bits of soldier to get Jakub's attention. He ran to the window and looked down at the road not imagining it might be Alan. As Jakub turned to walk away from the window a flat piece of Lego castle roof slammed against the window. Jakub looked across and saw Alan waving at him. Opening the window Jakub did that whispering through gritted teeth thing… "What are you doing??" "Trying to get your attention." hissed Alan back at him. Alan saw Mrs Snark's curtains twitch and move. He stepped back from the window and pointed to Mrs Snark's house raising his eyebrows to Jakub. The peering eyes of Alice Snark scanned the street.

CHAPTER EIGHT

Down at T's

Tom Rhodes stood in his shop. The sign above the door had been painted by his uncle Terry who had an A 'level in art from Derby College in 1996.

It proudly read Tom's Tins and Things. Tom had owned the shop since 2013. Well he rented it off Mr Chandray really who lived on the other side of town. Tom Tins sold everything you'd need after you'd been to Tesco and lost your list and came back to find you hadn't got what you wanted. Locals had shortened the name to Tom's Tins, then right down to Tom's and finally T's. And instead of going back to Tesco you'd walk around the corner to T's. It was more than you'd want to pay for stuff but convenient – he had thought of calling it 'Not cheap but close'. But Mr Chandray who knew about these things said it'd be a bad idea. Tom had just two trays of eggs left on the shelf, loads of everything else, not many tins of tomatoes, faded birthday cards and two packets of toilet rolls. The toilet rolls had just arrived in that morning, but even now he knew by early afternoon they'd all be gone. Three days ago Mrs Snark, whom Tom didn't really care for, came in and gave Tom a piece of her mind about how ridiculous it was that there were no toilet rolls. She stood there…. with an angry eyebrow dancing around on her forehead as Tom tried to follow her train of thought.

"If you, young man (Tom was 45) had an ounce of common sense there would be toilet rolls on that shelf. But you haven't, look at you, you could be supplying our need of wiping materials and sanitary salvation, but no you're probably spending all your time on Twitterface, or Insta-app, or Snapbook," her 'Scarborough's got talent' hat wobbled on her head.

"One thing is certain…" she said. "this street will have toilet rolls and I'm the woman to sort it." Tom took a deep breath as she left the shop, he knew she meant business.

A pigeon cooed on the very quiet pavement of Haddon Street, the wind blew gently and Alan sat on the edge of his bed carefully writing on a small piece of lined paper. "Jakub – something is going on. I need your help to unravel the bits of information I've got so far. Snark is talking to the Pygg's about something that involves shipments of rolls, maybe eggs, maybe salad, maybe forward rolls…who knows. But the truth is they're up to no good and at this time the country needs good." Sounded a bit dramatic the last bit, as he wrote he realised he didn't know very much, just had a bad feeling and a few words he'd heard. He finished it with… "You're the Snark expert…I'm relying on you!!"

He wrapped the message around a Lego brick and catapulted it into Jakubs garden.

The very next morning as Tom Rhodes opened his shop a white parcel arrived from the man in the van. Tom lifted it onto the shop counter; it wasn't heavy but quite bulky. Tom had been able to keep his shop open in these 'unprecedented times' because he was supplying much needed supplies to the area of Haddon Street Lower Bolsever.

Tom slid the scissors into the box. He loved the way Sellotape gave way to scissors. The easy tear as the scissors slid along. He opened the flaps. There inside were 60 toilet rolls. On top of the rolls was a piece of A4 paper with 'TAKE THESE AS A GIFT – SELL THEM AT THE HIGHEST PRICE – MORE WILL COME YOUR WAY' written on top. Tom shook his head and looked around him.

The shop was empty. No one around, just him and the sound of one car going past. "Sell them at the highest price, more will come." He sure could sell 60 rolls at this time. A pack of 16 was nine pounds and 25p. Where did someone get sixty rolls from at this time? He was mystified.

A little roll of information:

The use of toilet paper had been recorded in China as early as the 6th Century. The Chinese in the 14th Century had been producing thousands of rolls of paper and much of this had been scented.

The rest of the world seemed to have a different view on wiping – with the Europeans choosing rags, wood shavings, hay, stones, moss, water, snow, ferns, large leaves, plant husks, fruit skins, seashells or corn cobs. Good lord you'd need to be very desperate to use seashells!!

Joseph Gayetty is generally credited with the modern commercial availability of toilet paper. Introduced in 1857, he sold packs of flat paper with his name on it. Now in the USA you can get toilet paper with the face of Donald Trump printed on it – make of that what you will!!

Tom stacked the paper on his shelves. The price of ten pounds for six rolls seemed a little steep but these were hard times. I'm sure whoever sent them would show up with more thought Tom – little did he know they would show up and make some demands.

CHAPTER NINE

Someone's being naughty!!

The prime Minister sat in his chair looking out of the window. He'd just been standing on Downing Street clapping the country's carers and NHS. His hands felt quite stingy as he'd clapped and clapped. He took a big breath and thought "What a job this is…but what a job all those wonderful people who are saving lives are doing." On top of everything he also had Covid 19, bad cough, tight chest, sore throat the whole shebang. Boris wasn't a very patient man and liked to get things done. Great when things are going well, but not so great when you're trying to run a country from the confines of the apartment above 10 Downing Street. And throw into that mix a pandemic, the likes of which no one has ever seen. Well not unless you'd lived through the Spanish Flu of 1918. 102 years ago. There weren't many people alive who'd remember that. Boris gave a little cough and picked up the phone. "Hello is that Domino's Pizza… I'd like a large meat n spicy please. Yes, Boris is the name. 30 minutes is fine." He sat back and smiled to himself… "A man's gotta eat."

Jakub had spent the afternoon in the garden. He'd been giving some thought to Alan's message and wondered what the fuss was about. Maybe Mrs Snark had just been her usual rude self and upset Alan's family, as they'd run into her at Tom's Tins. He'd planned to get a reply to Alan later, he was trying to make a sort of catapult and copy the method Alan had used. Then it came to him, Alan and his dad loved to fish. Maybe Alan could get a rod from the garage, cast the line and a weight out of the bedroom into Jakub's garden and somehow Jakub could get that line to his bedroom and a quick communication system could be set up. Cunning plan!!

Jakub celebrated with a hard shot of his ball against the wall of the house. The ball hit the drainpipe and flipped high into the air. "Noooooooooooo!" shouted Jakub.

Yes–the ball once again arched into Mrs Snark's garden. Jakub ran indoors to his dad. "Dad, Dad come quick, no time to lose." Jakub explained the situation to his dad, who after having to buy many new footballs was as keen to sort the dilemma as quickly as Jakub. Jakub's dad had no appetite to go around and confront Mrs Snark…. as he said, "She was mustard." and he'd rather eat his own liver!

Jakub's dad had an idea – "You climb on the fence son. I'll get the ladders. Then I'll hold you by the ankles and hang you over the fence where you can grab the ball and I'll pull you back." If he'd have given just a few seconds to think this through maybe Jakub wouldn't have been so keen. He didn't. Jakub jumped up onto the fence and scanned the garden of Mrs Snark. All was clear and the ball was just a couple of feet from the fence. Jakub hung his body forward over the fence and his dad helped him slide forward, head first towards Mrs Snarks garden. Jakub's heart was banging out of his chest. He knew this was crazy and maybe not very well thought through…but at least his dad had him by the feet. As he hung in the air and reached for the ball Jakub heard the dreaded door click. He craned his neck to look forward.

The sight of Mrs Snark running down the garden in her tartan dressing gown made him swallow deep.

"Dad!" he shouted, "Pull me back…now!"

Keith pulled as hard as he could.

Mrs Snark shouted, "How dare you boy, you snivelling little pond life I'm going to give you the best slap you've ever had!!"

To be fair if Jakub had had the presence of mind he could have just slowed the whole thing down and said… "Excuse me Mrs Snark, but you'll find that scaring and slapping children in the year 2020 is very much frowned upon and could lead you to being prosecuted and possibly imprisoned."

He didn't have the presence of mind and to be honest thought he was going to die. He grabbed the ball; his dad went to pull him back over the fence but not before Mrs Snark had grabbed his arm. For an awkward moment Jakub and Mrs Snark were face to face across the fence. Her breath was much too close.

"Excuse me," he said "but social distancing laws don't allow for this … geeeeet offffff meeeee!!!"

Mrs Snark let go of his arm and strode purposefully back to the house.

She turned and looked at him with the angriest face that he had ever seen. Smoke began to rise from her ears; a hissing sound came out of her mouth. No words came, just the biggest sigh and growl ever.

Jakub's dad shouted, … "You are a very rude and bad tempered lady." His voice a bit shaky. It sounded like he wanted to be angry but it was that moment when anger in your voice is defeated by fear. The final word 'Lady' tailed off into a high-pitched squeak!!

Who wasn't afraid of Mrs Snark? Jakub and his dad stood and looked at each other. Relieved that they had the ball and were in one piece.

CHAPTER TEN

Just a feeling

Feelings are funny things. Neither Alan nor Jakub could prove anything was amiss on Haddon Street. To the outside world it was just another street in another town in a certain country that was going through a pandemic that was life changing. Yet these two boys had seen enough of the movements of Mrs Snark to set their feelings on high alert. Apart from being very nasty to Jakub's footballs and to Jakub himself and being generally rude to most people she met; there wasn't much they could accuse her of. But …something just didn't feel right. And when something doesn't feel right and that feeling doesn't go away, well you just have to make a plan.

Jakub headed back to his bedroom; he couldn't make the catapult work. Probably because he'd made one out of a wire coat hanger from his wardrobe. It just kept bending and snapping and his Lego bits fell into the front garden. He caught sight of Alan across in his bedroom.

With lightning speed he waved his arms … "Alan!" he shouted and waved. Jakub took out some paper and wrote single words…"STAND IN YOUR FRONT GARDEN". The two boys headed straight out the front door.

The distance between Alan's front garden and Jakubs is probably 35-40 feet. 10 metres. A double decker bus length. They stood looking at each other. We could walk out onto the street thought Alan and still keep to the rules of six feet or two meters apart. But it would look very suspicious. In fact they felt very suspicious now. Alan coughed:

"Hi, how's it going?"

"All good thanks Alan."

"Just wanted to ask you a quick question Alan. Have you ever fancied trying out your fishing rod, you know just practicing with it from your bedroom window?"

"Holy Curried underpants," thought Alan – "he's caught the virus and is going crazy".

He looked at Jakub with a face that said, "What is going on in your head?"

Jakub raised his voice a little more and began to speak out of the corner of his mouth…"Cast your rod upon the waters brother and I your friend will gather the line and verily bring it from the garden into my very own house and from there you and I will commune with nature, errrm and each other, kind of." He hadn't worked out the last part of his sentence and just garbled nonsense.

Standing in the garage again Alan grabbed the fishing rod and some line. Here goes again he thought. "Jakub my friend, something is fishy on Haddon Street and we are going to catch it."

Looking from left to right from his bedroom window Alan could see the coast was clear. "Walloping wafters," thought Alan – "I've done some funny things before but casting my fishing rod out of my bedroom window is on another level."

He could just get enough of a short swing that the lead weight would start to move. When he had enough swing he could flick it and unclick the reel mechanism. Then hopefully the weight would fly across the road and land in Jakubs garden.

"Here goes…"

As he flicked and let go, the weight flew across the road. With that swooshing sound it did when he fished with dad.

Halfway across a cyclist was passing.

A stranger, one of those many across the country that were using their hour's exercise to pedal as many miles possible. Bikes that hadn't seen daylight for years were dragged from the garage or shed. Dusted down if they were lucky and then hammered on the tarmac for mile after mile.

The lead weight caught on his bike frame with a clunk. The cyclist looked around and probably thought he'd hit a stone. The weight had wrapped around the frame. The fishing line began to unravel. Alan's eyes were so wide with shock they started to water. "What now?" he thought as the line whizzed out of the reel…if he keeps going I'll run out of line completely – if I flick the reel lock it may bring the cyclist to an abrupt end. Alan closed his eyes and flicked the reel lock on.

The strain started to pull though his arms. A lot. "Never had a fish like this." he thought. It got tighter and tighter and tighter. Alan's arms yanked forward, he found himself half hanging out of the window.

The cyclist was travelling down hill but the bike felt like it was going uphill. He stood up from the saddle and peddled harder. Alan's arms were now fully straining. "Arrrrrrrrgggghh."

In one sudden moment the line broke.

Alan fell backwards like a sack of spuds onto his bed. The cyclist found sudden speed. But not expecting it he shot forward and rolled over the handlebars. Good fortune offered the poor rider a soft bump as he hit a grass verge. Both Alan and the cyclist sat slowly upright thinking. "What was that?"

He reloaded the fishing rod with another weight, taking great care to get it right this time. With a flick of the wrist and great skill, the weight took off again and this time flopped beautifully onto Jakubs front lawn.

"Get in!" shouted Alan.

Jakub punched the air.

CHAPTER ELEVEN

Good people

Lottie sat back in her chair and let the BBC news wash over her.

"Today Captain Tom Moore walked with his walking frame around his own garden to raise money for the NHS." Lottie had heard something about this wonderful man. He was about to turn 100 and had planned to walk 100 laps of his garden. The TV and radio people had got behind the story and Tom's fundraising had gone crazy. Raising over thirty million of the finest English pounds to help the National Health Service. The people of Britain were all eyes watching as this man who should be at the end of his life was smashing it out of the park!! "Come on Captain Tom!" was the cry from the streets.

Lottie Pygg could feel that little stiffness in her back. She was 78 now and most days she felt a twinge here or there. Watching Captain Tom gave her two feelings. One that she wished she'd done something as big and helpful as that and two that it made her feet ache even thinking about it.

Lottie had lived in Derbyshire for most of her adult life. She never imagined she'd spend her whole life living with her brother Ron. Ron was just about to turn 80 in two months. Maybe she and Ron would celebrate the lifting of the lockdown on his birthday – one could only hope.

Lottie stepped into the garden. The wind blew a gentle tune through the trees as Lottie bent down to look through the crack in the fence. No sign of Alan today. She loved to watch him playing football; she'd been a keen supporter as a young girl. Her dad would take her to Derby matches. She'd never lost the excitement, as the ball was about to hit the net she always shouted 'Goal'. Lottie walked back into the house. Ron still sat watching the news. Seemed like all they talked about now was the 'Virus'. Lottie worried that…well to be honest she worried about everything. How Ron would cope if he got sick, how she would cope if Ron got sick. How Ron would cope if she got sick, how she would cope if she got sick. What if the food ran out and no one came to help. They had a delivery from Agehelp UK once a week and they had most things. She remembered her mum telling her stories of how they had managed through the war. Some weeks they didn't have enough food and tea ran short. It was a time where people had to stay close and help each other. This was in some ways similar but in other ways so very very different. Lottie had been so used to having lunch with her friend Agnes each Tuesday morning. Having Ron around to talk to was good, but he couldn't talk like Agnes.

Ron turned the TV off and sat looking at Lottie. "How did we get wrapped up in Alice Snarks little game Lots?" "When did we become those people?"

"What people?"

"You know those people who try to look after themselves when things get tough. We've just watched Captain Tom doing things to help other people. What have we done? …we've agreed to take 50p off every toilet roll that Alice sells. What have we turned into the Mafia…"

"Ron all I agree to was to let all our friends know that if they needed toilet rolls then we could introduce them to Alice."

"But we don't even know how she's getting all these toilet rolls when it seems no-one else can." Ron's voice swerved up at the end.

"Alice has a way of convincing you Ron, I've only sent a text to some friends and posted on Facebook twice."

"Ruddy Facebook Lottie." "You and Ruddy Facebook".

CHAPTER TWELVE

Plotting

"Gary, Gary is that you?" Alice Snark said into the telephone. She'd had the same phone for about 25 years. It was made of pale blue plastic, and made a trilling sound as it rang. They even called it 'The Trill Phone' back in the day. On this phone Alice had made the most important calls of her life. She'd rang the Vicar to tell him she wouldn't be coming back to church as she'd had a fall out with Mrs Simmons. She'd called the Sunday Times to tell them that the Vicar wasn't a very nice man as he'd told her to grow up and make friends again with Mrs Simmons. The Sunday Times journalist had said, "Mrs Snark we're a serious newspaper that covers world issues. You falling out with Mrs Simmons isn't going to light the imagination of Mr Average from Brixton over his breakfast reading." Mrs Snark just replied with…. "The world is full of small-minded people." And put the phone down.

Mrs Simmons had accused Mrs Snark of taking some of the food out of the Harvest Festival basket two years ago. "When I left the tins of beans and shortbread biscuits in the basket I expected them to go to the poor of Chesterfield." Mrs Simmons had said to The Vicar when she called him. "I came into the Church the following day and many things were gone. I saw Alice leaving as I walked up, with a bag." The vicar was left in a bad place, as he needed to speak to Mrs Snark about this. You can only imagine the problems he faced as he tried to manage the fall out. Mrs Snark had, to be fair, tried to go back to Church the following week. But the anger she felt was overwhelming. "Stealing, Stealing," she chanted to herself. "Does that woman know how hard it is to live on the money I have?" "The food is left there for the needy and deserving." Mrs Snark spent the whole service thinking of how she could get back at Mrs Simmons.

"I could leave some very strong glue on the seat where she sits at Church …and when she goes to leave .. I'll accuse her of stealing the seat!!!" Her blood was boiling.

Gary, Alice's son took a deep breath when he realised it was his mother on the phone. He was 55 years old and even now when he heard her voice his knees became a little weak and his heart pumped a little faster. "Hello Mother, yes it's me."

"Did you manage to do what I asked you to do Gary?"

"Yes Mother I did what you suggested." Gary said.

"Did anyone see you Gary?"

"No Mother, I took great care. I lifted the rolls out of the back door of the home and into the van. The driver is someone I've known for a long time. I've given him some money to keep quiet."

"Not too much money I hope Gary, we're trying to make some money here. This pandemic has destroyed my pension; it's also destroyed your inheritance. The house I live in Gary won't be worth very much after this and when I die you will be left with nothing."

Gary took another deep breath. He knew deep down that he shouldn't be involved in the theft of large amounts of toilet rolls from the nursing home he worked in. But his mother, who used to be a God fearing woman had now talked him into stealing. She had also somehow managed to get a supply chain across Derbyshire corner shops that would take the rolls and sell them to people at a much-inflated price. Mrs Snark knew she had a small window of time to sell as many rolls as possible before the supermarkets started supplying as normal.

According to Wikipedia panic buying is as follows:

Panic buying occurs when **consumers** buy unusually large amounts of a product in anticipation of, or after, a **disaster** or perceived disaster, or in anticipation of a large price increase or **shortage**.

Gary had been listening to a radio report that morning "It's actually a type of herd or sheep behaviour when people just do what other people do," said the reporter "it's monkey see, monkey do. What makes it worse is that there has never been a shortage of toilet rolls during this pandemic, but people make it feel like there's a shortage by buying large amounts …emptying the shelves and making other people panic."

As Gary and his mother spoke on the phone the TV blared in the corner of Gary's front room… "THE PRIME MINISTER BORIS JOHNSON HAS BEEN TAKEN INTO HOSPITAL."

Boris sat up in bed. Two nurses wearing masks gathered around his bed. Doctor Redmond who is the PM's own personal doctor sat on a chair next to Boris. "Boris this is just an advisory stay for you, hopefully it won't be too long and we'll get you back to Downing street," Boris rolled his eyes. "Dr Redmond, I'm here because I'm taking your advice, I'm a very busy man just now as you can imagine. I'm expecting a call from the USA, China, Chile, New Zealand and Australia. Just do what you need to do and get me back to Downing Street." Dr Redmond rolled his eyes, well hidden behind his mask and plastic visor.

CHAPTER THIRTEEN

Gunfight on the high wire

Tom had never had so much business. For the whole of that week the shop was as busy as the Friday before Easter and Christmas Eve. Tom remembered one Friday about five years ago, a dull December day. He'd popped out to get some more sprouts from the wholesaler, grab a coffee from Starbucks all timed to be no more than an hour. He dashed back and thought there may be one or two people milling around, waiting for him to open again. As he turned the corner Tom could see about twenty people queuing outside the shop. He later found out that Tesco had had a power cut and that there was a logical reason why he was bombarded. But at the time he felt a wave of stress come over him. The first few days of lockdown had been like that, he'd open the door first thing and a gaggle of people would be waiting. Many saying, "Did the toilet rolls arrive Tom?"

Tom had learned his trade as a shopkeeper well. He'd worked for Mr Chandray for about ten years in Normanton Derby. Mr Chandray had about four very successful shops all over Derby and knew every detail of the corner shop world. Mr Chandray would say "Tom, the best rule to learn in shop keeping is to serve the person in front of you. Ignore any sighs, tapping of fingers, rolling eyes, shuffling feet, loud coughs and so forth of any other people in the shop."

"But at the same time you have to have one eye on the tricky looking person who may be hiding behind the shelf and filling their pockets with Mars bars." "How can I possibly do that?" Tom remembers saying.

And all these years later Tom now has the ability to do just that. Like a very skilful footballer who instinctively knows where the ball is going to land, as they spin on their heel and pass the ball to someone yards away. Tom can juggle all of this. But day one of the lockdown was on another level.

As a very proud shopkeeper; he knew that his business was a direct result of the corner shops that had developed over a hundred years ago. Britain is not really a very big island and is often known as a nation of shopkeepers. It's a saying that was thought to be an insult that Napoleon came up with. Probably after he'd had a beating from the British Navy at the battle of Waterloo – a big insult.

Most of us can remember a time when we've needed the corner shop, buying some sweets, getting the paper for mum and dad. Beans when we've run out. That amazing bar of chocolate when we've got some spare cash after washing mum's car. The corner shop is amazing and now more than ever Britain needed its corner shops. And Tom was the man for the job. He caught sight of himself in the security mirror near the crisp shelf, pulled his tummy in and pushed his chest out. "Maybe I need a bit of training Tom." he said scolding himself.

As Jakub pulled the fishing line tight into his bedroom window, he just knew this was going to work so well. Alan watched across the street. He had tied his end to the window latch inside. The line being so thin meant he could close the window over it and all would be good. Alan reached out of the window and twanged the line. Nice and tight. The real test could be sending some Lego across. Alan looked at his Lego box. Just four years ago he'd started with one small box, a Lego boat that held a scuba diver. Making a small loop with a paperclip hooked over the fishing line nicely. This would hold a small plastic tub by the handle and allow them to send messages across.

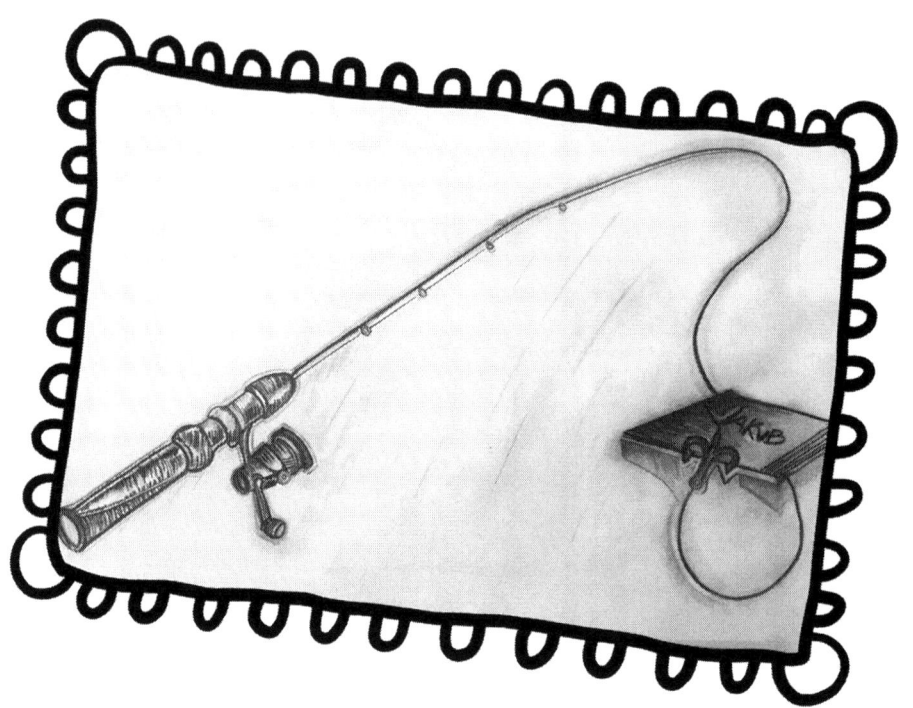

CHAPTER FOURTEEN
Gone fishing

That morning Alan had seen a delivery of a fairly large parcel to Mrs Snark's house, maybe around 10.30am. His dad Eric had left the house very early around 5.30am; he'd had a morning shift. Postal workers were doing a very important job – people felt so much better when they got a letter. Well as long as the letter was a nice one. Some people still were getting letters that were bills. Having to find money when they'd been laid off work, 'Furloughed.' The new word that people hadn't even thought of before all this – 'Furloughed.'

As he watched the parcel arrive, left at Mrs Snark's doorway, Alan got the feeling that the parcels were definitely all part of the strange arrangement that The Pygg's and Mrs Snark had going on. He couldn't get his head around how the Pygg's could be involved in something that wasn't truly right and proper. In fact he knew that he was inventing the facts here. For all he knew Mrs Snark could be having parcels of much needed food delivered and then sending them out to poor people. "I don't want to be cynical," thought Alan. "Have an open mind." But something deep inside didn't stack up.

Alan's house, sat slightly higher than Jakub's, so he could slide the message tub across to Jakub and it would gently roll down hill. But he needed to put another piece of line on it to pull it back. Alan's empty plastic fishing bait container has become the message tub. He'd untied the line and poked it through the handle. Then tied the other piece of line through it. He tried a dry run to Jakub's house, it slowly slid along and then became stuck about ten feet from Jakub's window. "It needs more weight," thought Alan. He pulled it back, took an apple sized pebble he'd brought back from Scarborough beach and popped it in.

"Shivering snifferwacks," thought Alan. "This should work!!" The tub sailed like a dream along the line, across the road and into Jakub's window. Jakub put a small chocolate freddo bar into the tub, waved to Alan and off it went. This is amazing thought Alan – who needs a mobile phone… so boring!! And no one can hack our messages …top secret.

As they practised sending sweets, messages and the odd piece of Lego the curtains at Mrs Snark's twitched and moved.

The front window opened and the grey barrel of an air rifle popped its nose out.

Alan sent a message across to Jakub.

"Jakub, I'm not sure what any of this means, but I've got a feeling that Snark is up to no good. The Pygg's gave away that Mrs Snark and they were up to something when I overheard them in the garden. They mentioned rolls and it sounded like they were smuggling something. I saw a parcel arrive this morning that looked quite big. I've nothing more to go on here. Can you keep your eyes open and we'll see what we can find out?"

Alan sent across the message – as it went a whistle and whizzing sound sizzled through the air.

Mrs Snark had taken a shot at the message tub. It missed. She loaded the gun again. This time just a few feet from Jakub's window the pellet from the gun hit fair and square. The tub spun around and the message dropped from the bucket. As it floated down to the ground Alan watched from behind his curtain.

Snark

The gun

The shot

The spinning of the tub

The message floating to the floor

He heard the cackling tones of Mrs Snark. That well-known cackle that made him shiver.

The message almost hit the ground – but not before a gust of wind caught it and blew it into the garden of Mrs Snark.

Now she would know that they were aware of whatever it was she was up to. Alan felt a wave of sickness flow through his stomach.

Her wide staring eyes were looking up at him. He peered from the window as Mrs Snark stepped out of her front door and went to retrieve the message.

"Well this is where it really gets interesting." thought Alan.

CHAPTER FIFTEEN

Bozza – Mr Johnson to you!

Alexander Boris de Pfeffel Johnson was born in New York in June 1964. You won't be surprised that he dropped the rest of his name and stuck to Boris. He'd been practising to be Prime Minister for years. Well centuries actually as his family had a very special connection to royalty and politics. His grandmother 'Granny Butter' (don't spread this story around!!) was a descendant of Prince Paul Von Wurtleberg, who was related to King George II. Which makes Boris related to the Royal Family in a distant kind of way. He's also related to loads of other royal families across Europe…so he's well connected.

Well you can be as well connected as you like…but when the 'big bully boy Corona 19 biffer bob' hits you …bang down you go!! And down Boris went down.

Lying on his back looking at the ceiling wasn't a popular position for Boris. He'd only just started the fight of his life as Prime Minister and now here he was well…fighting for his life. For many years he'd thought that maybe he could do the top job, the big cheese job, the leader job. And it had happened – he'd won. It's a funny thing winning. They do say be careful what you wish for. Sometimes you hope and wish and pray and struggle for something and when you get it, its totally different to what you thought it would be.

Just months after being appointed as PM Boris would be sat at his desk when the call came in. "Prime Minister Johnson," said one of his advisors "the Covid 19 new Coronavirus has really started to take hold in London."

They all knew that Italy and Spain and France were struggling to keep up, but not the UK, surely we'd be ok. Boris sat back in his chair. "We've got to have a really good plan," he thought, "we need the best scientists and doctors and NHS people and well jolly well everybody who can help get us through this pandemic." Boris looked at the picture of Winston Churchill on his desk. The wartime leader who'd managed to cajole, blag, bluff, plan and use anything he could think of to get Britain through the war….and win!! I need some Churchill spirit thought Boris; I need to think what Winston would do. Well Winston would do one thing a whole lot – he would speak to the country as often as he could through the radio. Winston's speeches were a way of him raising the courage of the British people. He would need to take people with him if he was going to win this war. Boris reached for his Churchill's speeches book on the shelf and flicked to his favourite one. "Never was so much owed by so many to so few." He'd read that many many times and it now meant so much to him.

"The gratitude of every home in our Island, in our Empire, and indeed throughout the world, except in the abodes of the guilty, goes out to the British airmen who, undaunted by odds, unwearied in their constant challenge and mortal danger, are turning the tide of the World War by their prowess and by their devotion. Never in the field of human conflict was so much owed by so many to so few."

The National Health Service was going to be Boris's weapon of choice.

The men and women who were so skilled at caring and looking after sick people would need so much support and encouragement, the whole country could get behind them. Cheer them on as they did their jobs. Boris knew he had the fight of his life here.

CHAPTER SIXTEEN

Beat this on the beaches

At that very moment, as Boris placed the book down on the table, before him appeared a great hulk of a man dressed in black with a walking cane.

Boris shook his head. He shook it again. Winston, yes the Winston Churchill stood before him. Just six feet away from Boris he stood as if making a point about the social distancing. Winston looked down at Boris in his bed.

"Boris…you're afraid," he bellowed.

"Fear will make you freeze and make you lose this battle."

…Winston was chewing his cigar as he said the words, bits of spit flying out all over Boris, "Good job you're a ghost," thought Boris. "or I'd be in trouble."

"Boris – remember, you've got to be bigger and more crazy than this virus. You have to never give in. But one thing that's going to be vital in this fight, is taking the people with you. Inspire them to do the right thing. Celebrate our National Health Service… cheer them on!!"

Boris sat with his mouth open and looked straight at Churchill expecting him to disappear in a puff of smoke. But he didn't.

"Well, well man…any questions?"

Boris had loads. But he couldn't think of them right at that moment. Then it came to him.

"Mr Churchill…" he stammered "one thing that has always made me wonder is …where did you find the courage?, the energy, the stubbornness to carry on, even though the Nazi's had us beaten, but…but, but you made them think that we were all waiting on the beaches to fight them?"

"…and by jove we would have fought them with spades and shovels and pitchforks and bare hands. We would never give in."

Winston's voice echoed through Boris' head.

The great wartime leader repeated the line he had said many years ago:

"I felt that all my past life had been but a preparation for this hour and for this trial."

"Boris – you will find this your biggest trial. You will almost come to join me beyond the clouds, death will want to drag you away too early… because it knows you're a fighter…. fight hard Boris and you will win."

With those words Winston strode out of the office door and slammed it behind him. Standing to his feet, still shaking Boris followed him. Looking down the corridor he heard the door onto the street slam.

He lay back down, looking at the ceiling. Death had tried to come and take him. "Be strong." Winston had said sternly to him. The nurses and staff at the hospital were working hard to settle his breathing and get him through this battle, not because he was the leader of the country. Although that probably played on their minds. But because they were about saving people and people mattered.

This was day three of intensive care. Boris could feel the energy coming back to his body. He lay back and fell asleep. As he woke, the room was dark. Just a glow from the nurse's desk light. Boris looked at the ceiling again, all still white and blank. He heard a deep breathing next to him.

Looking to his left, there sat Winston. Open shirt and more casual now.

"Young man… that was a close run thing there. You almost came to join me in the other world. Good fight Boris. Now when you get back to business remember …just keep doing the same plan…. get them to stay home, protect the NHS and save lives."

Boris sighed a deep sigh – it's one thing to defeat death and meet Churchill, another to convince the public to stay home for months on end.

Alan had his own fight to win. Deep down he knew that Mrs Snark was up to no good. He just knew deep down. But without evidence he wasn't going to win this fight.

But Mrs Snark now had his letter to Jakub.

She knew, that they knew, that she was maybe up to something that they didn't really know.

He sat watching the five o'clock news briefing with his dad. "Boris Johnson has come out of intensive care," the reporter spoke confidently into the camera. "The Government and the whole country send him their best wishes and a continued speedy recovery." Alan knew Boris had a long journey ahead of him; he'd seen him clapping the NHS and didn't like the look on his face.

Just a few hundred yards away, Tom is opening another box of toilet rolls. On his security camera outside the shop a recording had been made. His phone alerted him at 5am that morning. The camera played the footage of a person in a green shooting style jacket, with a cap on that says something about Scarborough. He can't quite make it out. As Tom opened the shop at 8am the box sat by the door. He pulled it in. The phone rang. "Hello Tom's Tins and stuff," he answered. "Listen very carefully," a voice hissed. "…I know you sold the last box of rolls at a good price, a very good price." "So sell these and I'll come and introduce myself – no need for secrecy after you've sold these…. I'll come and collect the money." The phone clunked down at the other end. Tom looked up and thought "what have I done."

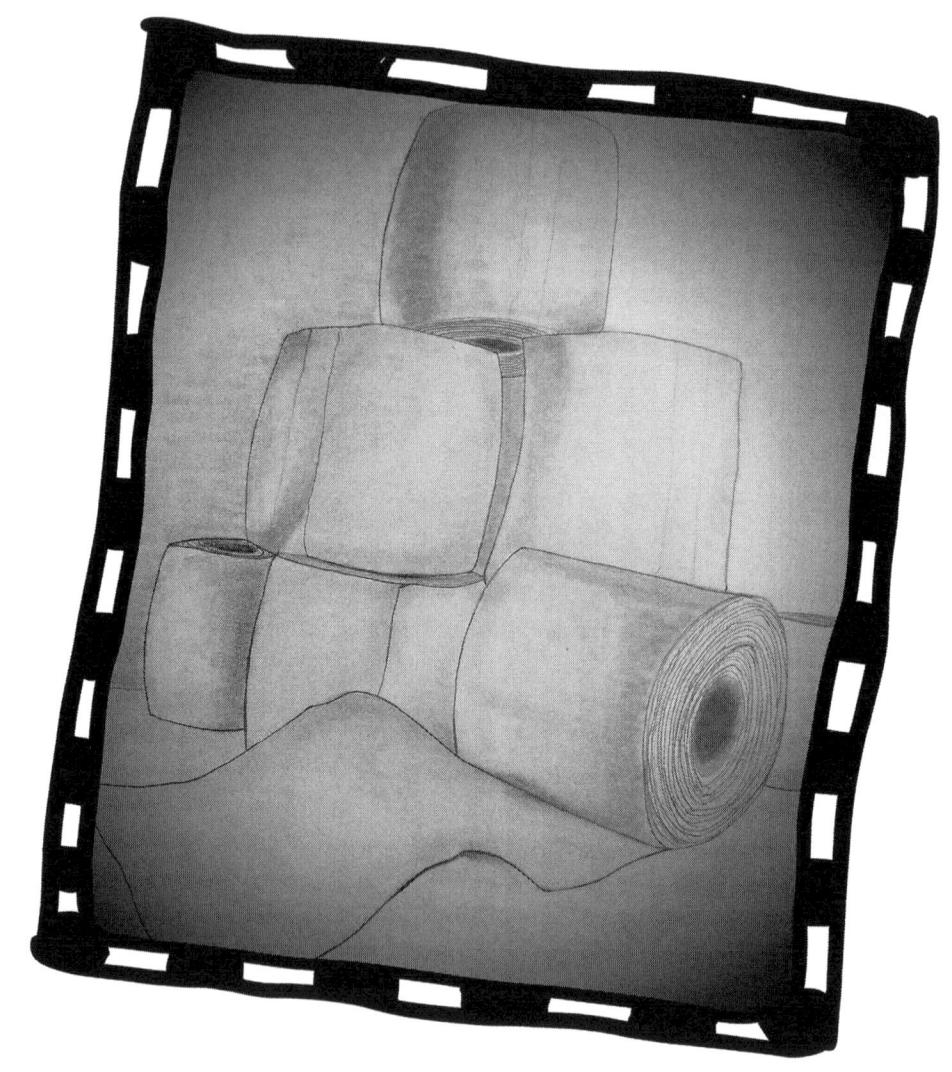

CHAPTER SEVENTEEN
Sorry not sorry

Gary Snark had now taken two boxes of 60 toilet rolls from the Nursing home. For the mathematicians out there, it equalled 120 rolls. They had a whole storeroom filled with all kinds of goodies, well mainly wipes and cleaning products. Gary worked as a porter and odd job man; he could do a pretty good job at fixing most things. He wasn't sure where this bad side came from, he earned enough money, had been a happy kid, when his mum wasn't being strange. He generally wanted to be good. He enjoyed life. But if he saw something that wasn't nailed down he kind of thought he could, well you know, lift it and make a few quid.

Gary had a good boss Mr Gibbons, he treated Gary well. Which made Gary feel even worse when he took the toilet rolls. But his mother Alice had a strange kind of logic about stealing these things.

"Gary,"

She would say

"At the end of the day, when all is said and done, in the grand scheme of things…"

"Gary,"

She would say,

"This is all going to be flushed down the big white pan, the bog, the toilet."

She'd seemed so sensible when he was a boy. Helped him with his homework, cooked nice food, his favourite spaghetti bolognaise. But when he left home and his sister Janice had become ill and eventually needed to be in hospital for many months then sadly, very sadly died. His mum Alice became a little strange.

He knew she'd fallen out with the lady at church and after that stopped going and started writing to newspapers about the vicar…it was all so sad. But Gary thought, "I need the money and a few quid for toilet rolls is all very welcome."

On the afternoon that Gary decided to take the last box of rolls, the home was all very quiet. The staff were taking tea around to all the elderly people as they rested in their rooms. The matron, Mrs Carney, was in her office, the owner Mr Gibbons was in his office calling around to suppliers of PPE Personal Protective Equipment. His home wasn't having too much trouble finding supplies, but if he didn't get in the queue for equipment he could be left with nothing. Two residents had tested positive for the virus and Gary was nervous about being at the home that day.

He slipped quietly into the storeroom. He'd called his contact with the van, the one who delivered all of the Amazon goods in the area. It was a simple case of just dropping the parcel outside his mum's door and she did the rest.

Gary knew the public desire for toilet rolls would run out very soon, but they could move on to other things he could get his hands on. Gary's way of making sense of his actions was "This is a war zone, we're in hard times and you've got to think quick and act on your wits…it's a black market."

Just a week earlier the French police near Paris had seized 140,000 facemasks that were supposed to be going to the health care workers and were about to be sold on the black market – an illegal underground system where people sell illegal and stolen items. They caught a man red handed unloading them from a lorry just north of Paris. These were strange times and people do wicked and strange things. (Incidentally the phrase red handed was started in Scotland around the 15th century, for people found with blood on their hands. The guilty!!…just in case you fancied knowing.)

The van arrived at the back door of the home, Gary waited with the box by the door. The van door swung open and Gary threw the box to Vance the driver, he swiftly loaded them and off to Alice's he sped. As Gary turned to walk back into the home Matron Mrs Carney stood behind him. Gary's heart almost stopped.

"Hi Mrs Carney, you all ok?" stammered Gary.

"Yes I am Gary, who was that?"

"Well I'd arranged for a friend with a van to come and take away some of that waste cardboard." he lied…face almost catching fire with shame. The cardboard had been building up and he'd been asked to deal with it.

Mrs Carney…. a trusting and lovely soul just smiled and turned back to her office. "You make sure you get some rest Gary, you've been putting in lots of hours this past week." Gary's shame and guilt almost exploded. Inside his head the voice of conscience was screaming loud. Which is really like your own little policeman tapping you on the shoulder and saying, "Hey what's going on in here?" You see many people don't think we need a God to tell us what's right and wrong, a king or president or policeman – we kind of have our own internal voice, if only we listen to it. Gary was virtually putting his fingers in his ears and shouting lalalalalallal…!!!

CHAPTER EIGHTEEN

Scary times

The van pulled up outside of Mrs Snark's house. She sat in the lounge window seat reading again the note that Alan had sent to Jakub...well tried to send. "Mrs Snark up to no good," she scoffed. "Up to no good. I'm trying boy, to take the excess toilet rolls out of the hands of those do gooder care home people and get them to the people who need them, and along the way add to my bank account."

She pursed her lips... "some people are clueless."

The door tapped. She saw the van drive away and the box left on the step.

She brought the box in, "Just a nice little Amazon order." at least that's what the neighbours thought. She moved the box into the hallway, looking back through the door she saw Alan at the window. Mrs Snark waved up at him. He dived behind the curtains. At that moment she decided how she would silence him.

Fear

Full on fear!

"Hahahahahaha"...she cackled.

"Fear in the middle of the night was the only way to deal with that boy. And what better night to do it than tonight. A full moon."

Alan had been catching up on some reading after watching Britain's Got Talent with his mum and dad. The stand out act had been a man on a unicycle holding his dog above his head whilst drinking a pint of water. The dog, called Geezer a cocker poodle, had a look on his face as if to say, "I could have been a guide dog or herding sheep or anything." The poor creature stood by the man's side ...who called himself Trevor Trapeze. Simon said to him "So can you win Trevor?" "Yes I can, I want to entertain the Queen and the whole world and everything. I promise you one thing Simon; if I come back you'll see a new spectacle. There's fire involved next time."

The dog, who had a slightly world weary face, looked up at Trevor… (who's real name was Ivan) and shook his head. The dog had seen Trevor burn his own hair badly three times now. He couldn't believe he'd just promised Simon to do the fire trick.

"You've got three yeses… hurray." "Hurray indeed thought the dog."

Alan lay on his bed and fell into a deep sleep. He didn't often have vivid dreams. Sometimes nice dreams where he was eating chocolate. They were so real that he tried to stay asleep even when waking up. The taste of chocolate was so real, he could feel himself chewing. But the best dreams were always the ones where he could fly. He'd step out of the house, take a little leap and he would lift just a few feet off the floor. Realising he could fly, he would will himself to go higher, just a few feet. It was as if he knew he shouldn't really be able to fly but he could and the energy and magic would only allow him just a few feet up. In other dreams he was right up with the trees. He could feel the wind on his face as he lifted a good twenty or thirty feet and then high above the trees. If he relaxed he could just float, his arms feeling the lightness under him. The space between himself and the floor was almost sponge like. Just his own mind was keeping him there. In one dream Alan rolled onto his back and stared at the sky. The clouds drifted by, blue skies lay thick behind him calling to him. Alan pushed up and soared high into the atmosphere – he ran and stepped onto clouds. They held his weight and he jumped from one to another. Knowing he was pushing his luck Alan fell forwards and glided back down to his garden. He tried to land but couldn't, hovering just a few feet off the ground. Willing himself to land didn't work. He was stuck just a few feet off the ground. What had started out as Alan drifting off and thinking about his old dreams had turned into Alan falling asleep and having this new dream. He was stuck. His bedside light was on and the glow from this flickered on his face.

From outside his window a scuffle could be heard. Falling asleep so quickly had meant he hadn't closed his curtains or got undressed.

A shadow of a woman's head fell across his bed. The shadow moved slightly but was very still, watching.

CHAPTER NINETEEN
The ladder of success

The Pygg's had a small role in the toilet roll fiasco. They were to keep an eye out for anything suspicious and let their friends know when rolls were available. Mrs Snark knew that they would be watching her most days as their level of nosey was set to number 11 on the nosey dial.

Doing that whispering and hand movements across the street sign language type of thing was how she communicated. Lottie had managed to get some orders from a few friends, not many. In the last chat across the street Alice had planted an idea. Lottie hadn't a clue where she'd got the idea.

If she had understood correctly Alice Snark seemed to be saying, "If you can get more orders from your friend's Lottie, there may be some money in this. I know your pension doesn't pay much and you and Ron could use the money."

"Money." Lottie hadn't even thought of that. But she sure could use some more money. She put the thought to the back of her mind.

Jakub lay on his bed that night, reading. The night of Alan's dream. The wind was blowing outside. He'd thought he could hear a scraping sound, but put it down to the wheelie bin blowing in the driveway.

A dark shadow moved across Alan's garden. The shadow was carrying a small extendable ladder. The shadow, the shape of a stooped elderly woman moved towards the wall and rested the ladder against it. Pulling a small string could extend this lightweight ladder. It was a very useful tool for older, less strong people. But tonight Alice Snark was putting to use a ladder designed to reach the top of a cupboard not a bedroom window. The ladder would just reach, but became wobbly. It rose up as you pulled the string hard. It reached just to the bottom of Alan's window. It was 3am.

Alan had moved into that REM sleep state (Rapid Eye Movement sleep), where the person dreams very very deeply. Apparently only mammals/humans and birds sleep like this. Tonight Alan was in that technical term 'away with the fairies'. He looked so angelic as he slept. He'd moved on from the flying dream and was now very much into a problem solving dream sequence. He could see his friend Jakub had been captured by Mrs Snark. She had tied him to a lamppost outside on the street, wrapped him up tightly with toilet rolls…but this was such tough toilet roll that Jakub was completely stuck. The dream version of Mrs Snark was super strong about seven feet tall and able to pick cars above her head with one hand. She'd picked a big van up above her head and was about to drop it onto Jakub. "You boy have kicked just one football too many over my garden and the end has come."

In the dream Jakubs parents stood outside their front door on their hands and knees begging Alice Snark not to do it. "Please spare Jakub, he's such a lovely boy. "

Mrs Snark looked at them with huge anger in her eyes and shouted "Never!!!."

Alan felt a wave of anger come over him. "Holy hot dogs and smashed bananas." he cursed. He could never allow the evil Mrs Snark to hurt his friend. He ripped off his pyjama jacket and revealed a t-shirt that had a big letter A on just in the same style as Superman would wear. He jumped into the air to fly as he had done just minutes before and fell flat onto the road. Bumping his head. Mrs Snark roared with laughter. "You stupid pig-headed, nincompoop!" she shouted. "Yes NINCOMPOOP." It was almost as if everyone on the street stopped to look at her. "NINCOM-POOP?" everyone shouted…"Who says NINCOMPOOP?" Mrs Snark unfazed by the ridicule screamed again at Alan… "You'll never save him." The white van hurtled towards Jakubs body as Alan tried frantically to fly to the rescue.

The world of dream and reality collided in one sensational moment. Alan, still in a dream state, jumped up onto his bed and spun around to face the window. He'd now half woken himself up as he shouted

"Noooooooo" at the window…

Just at the same time as Mrs Snark appeared at the top of her ladder.

To say she was shocked was an understatement. Alice Snark was wearing a mask, a nasty clown mask and in her hands she clutched a hand written sign, which read, "Stay away from Mrs Snark or you will suffer." It all happened too quickly to really understand. Jakub had opened his curtains to see what the fuss was; Lottie and Ron ran out into the street wondering if they were missing something, maybe the bin. Alan stood on the bed…the clown mask didn't scare him as he was already in flight or fight mode. He shouted again

"No Mrs Snark. No."

CHAPTER TWENTY

Heaven is just a step away

Alice Snark gripped the top of the flimsy ladder. The boy she'd climbed this ladder to scare the living daylights out of, flew towards the window. His face a mass of anger and fear and rage. His eyes span in his head like monster cartoon eyes. Startled she lost her balance. The easy flip up ladder became an easy flip down ladder. Alan watched as Mrs Snark arched backwards, the ladder wobbled, Mrs Snark shouted "Hhhhhheeeeellllp."

Alan tried to reach towards the window. Nothing he could do would help. For just a few seconds the ladder left the side of the building and wobbled free from everything. She held tight to the top. Wiggling her hips seemed to keep it in one place. Then gravity took its own course of action. For one moment it seemed as if the ladder would fall forwards to the wall. Then it changed its mind!!

Mrs Snark and the ladder toppled backwards and landed solidly onto the roof of Alan's dads car.

A 1999 Blue Ford Focus 1.8 litre with Alloys. The crunch was sickening.

All was quiet for what seemed like an hour.

Alice Snark, whom Alan's mum Jane described as a very sad and angry 79 year old lady – lay very still.

The roof of the car creaked in the night air.

Just a long groan came from her lips.

Like a wounded tiger she lay helpless.

No one else moved.

An owl hooted.

A cat yawned.

In the distance you could hear the train from Derby to Sheffield pass by. Probably taking mail and stuff. The front door to Alan's house opened and out stepped Eric. Jane stood behind him. She whispered in his ear

"Don't forget to keep six feet apart Eric."

Eric just gasped

"My car".

Not the best and most caring response, but honest at least. From his viewpoint all he could see was a person in a shooting jacket with a 'Scarborough's got talent' hat, wearing a clown mask, in the huge dent on his car.

As the ambulance made its way down Haddon Street, Alan, Lottie and Ron, Eric and Jane stood close to Alice Snark watching her. They could hear the siren, the blue lights getting closer. Lottie had checked on Alice and she was breathing, in fact she was saying things like "stay away from me you silly people, let the professionals deal with this." They could see she was in pain but still almost conscious enough to be snarky.

The ambulance driver climbed out of the vehicle. Dawn and her colleague Chris the Paramedic had just worked a full shift. After attending many calls about Covid 19 they were intrigued to find an elderly lady flat on the roof of a Ford Focus. "Hello sweetheart," Dawn said… "how've you got yourself here?"

Eric closed one eye waiting for an angry reply from Mrs Snark. But by now she'd fainted and needed to be helped into the ambulance. Dawn and Chris carefully and gingerly lifted the now quiet Alice off the car. They placed Alice on a stretcher and carefully slid her in the back of the ambulance.

Alan was surprised at how much equipment was in the back of the ambulance and how calm Dawn and Chris were.

Everybody in the street went back to bed and Alan and his mum and dad went into the house. Alan told them all about the dream and how he'd wanted to save Jakub. He tried to go back and fill them in on the fishing rod and the note and The Pygg's… "Woahhhh." said his dad quite loudly.

"Alan its now 4am, you're very tired and none of this is making sense. Go to bed and we need to call the police because our car has been damaged and an old lady has hurt herself badly trying to climb a ladder to your window in a clown mask." Eric looked at Jane… "Not sure how to explain all of this to the police."

The next morning Gary had a call from the hospital to go and see his mum who'd had a fall. All sounded very innocent thought Gary. Maybe she's been trying to chase that kid out of her garden again. Annoying kids, glad he'd never had any of his own.

CHAPTER TWENTY-ONE

Not all bad

As she lay in the back of the ambulance, her head felt like a sack of potatoes that had been dropped off a bridge. Not that she had a clue what a sack of potatoes falling felt like. A feeling of loneliness came over her. "Where was Gary now?

Would they tell him here she was? How would they contact him? That stupid boy had run at the window and scared her so much her head span. Why had he done that? Did he know that she was going to scare him and got there first? Ooooh she was so mad. She could spit!"

Dawn drove the ambulance and Chris sat in the back with Alice to make sure she was ok. Chris wore the biggest mask and plastic gloves; Alice wondered if this was how the world was always going to be. The siren wailed eawww eawww eawwwww into the night sky.

Across the country and around the world many ambulances, 1000's of ambulances were carrying people to hospital. English people, Scottish people, Indian, Norwegian, American, Canadian, Irish, Australian. So many countries and so many people.

The word UNPRECEDENTED had been used so much that it joined the ranks of things that were unprecedented. The unprecedented use of the word unprecedented. Unparalleled, record, extraordinary, unique, first time, unmatched. These poor words didn't get a sniff in. Unprecedented was king of words!!

As Alice's ambulance arrived at the hospital it joined a queue of ambulances that sat waiting to deliver its occupants. She hadn't been to hospital for many years. The last time was when her big toe became infected after she'd kicked the kitchen door by accident. The pain was so bad that she fainted and banged her head on the floor. Gary had telephoned, he'd called and called that day and came around about three hours later to find her on the floor. Here she was again, back at the hospital.

The morning after the fall, Eric sat in the lounge with Alan and two police officers. They were a good six feet away.

"So run that past us again Mr Sheen." said officer Shrimp. Officer Shrimp was about 40 years old and had taken his hat off to reveal an interestingly baldhead. He still had hair all around the sides like a monk, but had kept some hair at the front of his head, which he'd grown and gelled back over the more baldy bits. Eric was drawn to look at the hair whilst Officer Shrimp spoke. "Well…" said Eric… "we now know it was Mrs Snark, but last night all I saw was a person in a clown mask. Lay on top of my car she was, dented the roof she did. And smashed the front window of the car and she was groaning. Very loudly and then she stopped."

"Why do you think she was up a ladder outside your room?" said the Officer as he looked at Alan.

Alan's mind was doing its own little movie show at this time. He could see himself jumping up onto the bed, to shout at Mrs Snark in his dream, then seeing her in a clown mask outside his room in real life. Falling backwards onto his dad's car. Then the ambulance came to get her. Alan opened his mouth to start to make sense of all of this to the Officer but the words didn't flow very well. He wondered if he was guilty of scaring Mrs Snark off the ladder and causing her injuries? So much to think about.

"Well Officer, I saw Mrs Snark, what I mean is she's been acting a little strange. I sent a note to my friend Jakub across the street. She saw the note and managed to get it from us. And then after she'd seen the note she got even stranger."

The Officer had started to write some things down, and then he put his pen down. "You're not really sure what's going on are you son?"

"Why you sending a note to your friend should end up with an old lady up a ladder outside your window in a clown mask at 3am is beyond any of us. Now make sense." At this point Alan was pretty sure that he was going to be arrested. As luck would have it the Officers radio crackled into life.

"Control to Shrimp, Control to Shrimp."

"Go ahead this is Shrimp." "Hi Shrimp – There's a nasty lorry accident on the A6 just towards the Matlock turnoff." Shrimp fired back a reply. "I'll be there as soon as possible." He turned to Alan "Listen son, make sure you think long and hard about what happened, I'll be back and will need the full story. Your dad's car has been badly damaged, an old lady is in hospital and you're the only one who seems to know anything."

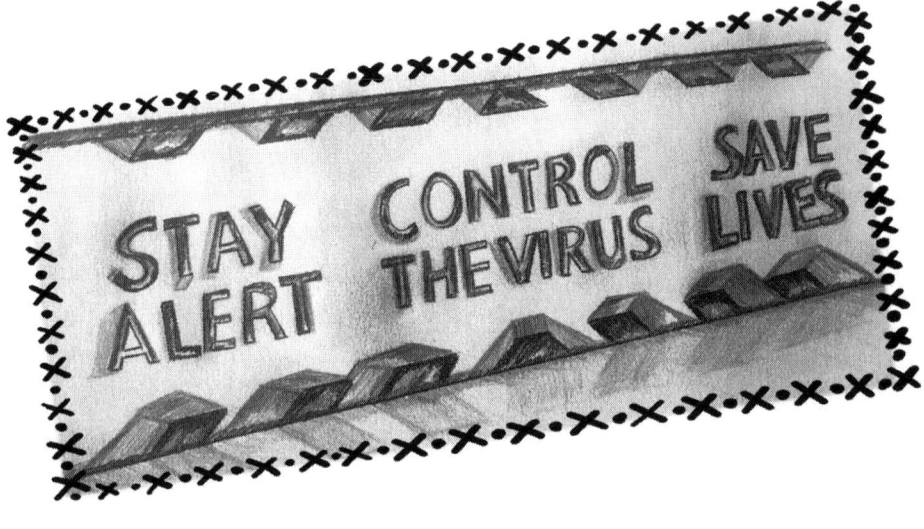

CHAPTER TWENTY-TWO
More good people

Tom had more toilet rolls than any other shop in the area. They were selling fast. He was happy with the business but felt very uncomfortable with what was going on. The message that someone was going to come and say hello, collect some money and do other deals maybe felt very dodgy. He would just have to wait for the mystery person to show up and see what happens.

The policeman had gone on his way to the incident, Alan had gone to his room to get his story straight and Eric sat on the sofa and clicked on the TV.

"The Prime Minister is now out of hospital and back at his home Chequers."

Gushed the ITV reporter from behind her desk.

Chequers is a country house that was given to the Government by a wealthy man back in 1921. It's about 40 miles from London. This was a good place for Boris to get better before he led the second biggest fight of his lifetime.

"Mr Johnson has praised the NHS for saving his life."

The reporter glanced down at her notes; "He has named some of the nurses and is very very grateful."

Eric felt a wave of relief come over him.

The last thing you need in a pandemic is the leader of the country dying from the wretched bug. Eric had spent the last few weeks seeing all the fearful and confused faces of people behind their windows. People shouting at him… "Leave the parcel on the doorstep and I'll come and get it when you've gone." Eric had felt like they saw him as a possible carrier of the disease, someone they couldn't trust.

One elderly lady Mrs Tanner, about 97, lives in Squires cottage, a lovely old place in the country. She would appear at the window with a sign for him each morning.

She would write words of poetry, some quotes from world leaders and from the Bible that she thought would be good for Eric.

Endurance is one of the most difficult disciplines, but it is to the one who endures that the final victory comes. – Gautama Buddha

Jesus said… **With man this is impossible, but not with God; all things are possible with God.**

Vince Lombardi. "**Winning isn't everything, it's the only thing**."

Eric wasn't a religious man in any way. His great uncle Victor had been a Vicar of St Thomas in a local village. Eric didn't give much thought to God and spiritual things. But this pandemic had made him think. He'd been thinking a whole lot as he drove around the streets with letters and parcels. He was the messenger of all kinds of news. Some good, some bad. At Christmas he brought wonderful gifts and cards from all across the world. Spreading joy. He'd delivered the letter from Boris as he told the country his thoughts and how we were going to get through this. He was also maybe the bringer of the virus if he didn't strictly wash his hands and make sure he stuck to the plan of social distancing. Eric thought that this was going to be a big wake up call for the world. Things would be different. Families were missing each other, they loved each other and couldn't hug, couldn't play games with each other. So many people were finding new ways of being close. Playing games on line and maybe sending emails and Zoom calls and Facetime and Houseparty. You didn't have to be religious to know that good things were starting to happen in the world thought Eric. Maybe, even in the middle of all this horrible death and loss, people could still find hope and maybe the world could breath again and slow down.

Eric smiled as he thought of Mrs Tanner. How kind to write the note for him.

Gary called the hospital to find more information about his mother. It dawned on him that he couldn't even visit.

CHAPTER TWENTY-THREE

Smoking…

As Gary drove to St Barts home he was deep in thought. The roads were quiet. The birds were singing and the sky was a clear blue. It was just after 8.30am a beautiful April spring day. One white strip of jet stream whipped across the blue sky.

A Boeing 777 plane sped to Heathrow airport London. The seats were all empty of passengers but filled with cardboard boxes. The boxes filled with personal protective equipment for the UK hospitals. Some of that equipment would later arrive at Gary's care home. For now it flew six miles above the earth. From the cockpit the pilot could see a world below him that still turned in the same way. Still angled at 23.5 degrees, still span at 1,000 miles an hour still circled the sun and was circled by the moon. From his seat he could pretend that all was ok. Below him things had changed and maybe forever.

Gary Snark had made this journey of just five miles for a few years now. He loved the feeling of knowing how the day would play out. He'd arrive at work, make a cup of tea, make one for anyone else who was around and then start to work on the jobs that needed doing. Sometimes a tap that needed fixing other times helping with more difficult to fix problems. Like Joan's problem noises in her room.

"Gary," she'd say "there is definitely a tiger living under my bed and it keeps roaring at me in the night." Joan was in the early stages of dementia and would hear things that were real to her, maybe not heard by other people. Gary would lie under the bed whilst Joan stood at the doorway. "Can you see it Gary, is he scratching you?" Gary had a nice way of helping Joan to live with the tiger, "Let's call him Tony, Joan…he's a friendly tiger."

Gary turned the corner to the road on which St Barts home stood. He was stopped in his tracks by plumes of smoke coming from the roof and flames licking from the windows. He could hear screams that echoed through his car windows.

At this precise moment Alan appeared, cycling just a few yards behind Gary. He'd been doing his daily around the block bike ride. Working out in his muddled mind what he was going to say to Officer Shrimp. "What could he possibly say, nothing made sense. An old lady had dropped off a 'chuffing' ladder outside his bedroom window and he didn't know why."

St Barts home lay just one mile from his house. He saw a plume of smoke in the distance, wondered if someone was burning old furniture, it smelled awful. As he came closer the flames came into view. A loud cracking sound punched the air. He pulled his bike to a halt right next to Gary's car. They'd never met. Gary put his car back in gear and pulled a few yards forward and abandoned the car by the curb. He ran as fast as he could towards the home.

Alan threw his bike down and followed. "Suffering piddle pots." thought Alan. He hadn't a clue what he could do but instinct kicked.

Gary reached the glass front door in seconds; he kicked at it with his full strength. He'd refitted the door just three weeks ago, as it had been a little rotten. "Great," he thought, "trust me to do such a good job!!"

On the third kick a creak and a crack started to happen. The door gave way. By this point Alan had arrived at his side. Gary passed Alan his phone, "Dial 999 kid and do it fast."

Alan made the call.

Gary disappeared into a hallway of smoke. He coughed and fell backwards clutching at his eyes that were now stinging. He took off his hoodie and wrapped it around his nose and mouth, grabbed his sunglasses from his pocket and headed back in. "Anything to stop the smoke."

"Hello, hello?" said Alan,...

"Yes fire brigade please I'm at St Barts Home, it's on fire, a man has gone in. It's very bad." "Now slow down please," said the operator on the other end of the line.

"Tell me slowly where you are."

Alan managed to gather his breathing and push down the feeling of panic that was filling his chest.

"Erm it's at the end of Haddon Street near the Old Rectory house."

"Yes yes I can see the address here on my screen," said the operator. "Stay calm we'll have someone to you very soon."

Alan stood back as smoke poured out of the doorway. As if appearing from a ghost story, four or five soot covered elderly people started to stream out of the door. Alan could hear Gary's voice behind them – "Straight on Maude, Joan, Peter, straight on." They came out coughing and stood in the driveway. People from the surrounding streets began to appear with blankets and hot drinks.

CHAPTER TWENTY-FOUR

Clark Kentish and superish

Inside Gary had managed to open the door at the end of the lounge area and helped people to get out that way. The fire alarm sang like a screeching baboon.... a frightful sound that rang in his ears. He'd now seen Matron Carney and Mr. Gibbons dashing around helping people out of rooms and pushing open doors. He could see that the fire was coming from the store cupboard where all PPE and other equipment were kept. Including the cardboard that he should have sent to the rubbish pile. Gary pushed that thought to the back of his mind; he had a bigger job to attend to. It seemed like the fire had spread to the four upper rooms where according to Matron Carney one person was still in their room. "We can't get past the smoke," said Matron.

"It keeps pushing us back." Mr Gibbons looked terrified.

Gary placed his hoodie under the nearest tap he could find and soaked it through. He then wrapped it around his face and headed to the stairway. The smoke billowed down at a horrible speed. He could feel the heat up there.

"Wait till the fire brigade get here!" shouted Mr Gibbons, "Please Gary wait." He looked back and simply said, "There isn't time." As Gary took each slow step up the stairs the siren of the Fire engine could be heard, out of sync with the St Barts alarm. Mr. Gibbons shouted again "Gary wait wait!"

Reaching the top of the stairs and wrapped in suffocating smoke, Gary could just see the room ahead of him. He ran and pushed it open. Empty. He stumbled to the next room. Empty. He could hear a low groaning as he reached the next door. He pushed it open; Olga lay on the bed with her face covered by the sheets, smoke whirling around her head.

Olga had lived in that room for five years. Her few things she loved either on the walls as pictures or in draws for safekeeping. Gary recognized at once that Olga needed serious help and quick. Gary tried to wake Olga but she seemed half asleep, moaning and groaning. He felt his heartbeat rising as the panic set in. If he didn't get Olga to help soon she would die. Gary tried to lift Olga from the bed and help her to walk but she lay in a tight ball and it was hard to move her. Smoke whirled around the two of them.

Crack. Thud, Thud Whack.

A fire axe broke through the window. The fresh air flooded into the room. The woman behind the mask spoke sternly as she smashed the glass out of the whole window frame. "I'm coming in, everything's gonna be ok, help me with the lady." Teresa as Gary would later find out her name to be stepped into the room. Gary hadn't been able to wake Olga. She seemed still and lifeless. The smoke from outside of the door, where he'd closed it behind him, was held back by the fire seal on the door. But the heat was building up so much that Gary could hear the twisting and cracking.

Teresa took hold of Olga and placed her over her shoulder, Gary watched in awe as Olga was lifted onto the ladder and carried down. "Follow us when we've reached the bottom." said Teresa. The door cracked loudly and the room started to shake.

Alan stood in the car park placing blankets around the shoulders of elderly people. His mum called them the golden generation. People from the streets around were there offering help and support, coffee, tea, cake, biscuits. Alan wondered if this was how the war felt for his past family. A generation he never knew, going through tough times, making things work when all around was broken and damaged. Always brewing tea and making cake and putting a strong and caring hand around people.

Gary stood at the window and placed his leg over the side, the ladder seemed a little unsteady. As he started to climb down a huge ripping explosion hit his chest and blew him off the ladder and crashed him through the neighbours' fence.

A very blackened and battered Gary lay still. Above his head many miles high the sun slipped from behind the clouds and lit his sooty face.

Blood trickled down his cheek and the fire crew ran to pull him from out of the pile of fence boards.

CHAPTER TWENTY-FIVE

High praise indeed

Boris stood at the podium at 10 Downing Street. The union flags stood behind him. Perfectly folded and still. If they fluttered or moved you would know that someone had opened the front door at Number Ten Downing Street. A single TV camera stood in front of him. To his right was a huge Tv screen that linked straight to the laptops of journalists from across the UK.

Boris had no clue what any of these questions would be. On some days the journalists all asked the same questions.

"How long can people carry on like this?"

"How will people get paid?"

"Can we still see our parents if they are over 70?"

"Will the country run out of money?"

"Britain, you know how close things came for me. It was a very close call and with the amazing help of the NHS doctors and nursing staff they pulled me through. I will be forever grateful. Now I'll hand you over to Doctor Chris Whitty Chief Medical Officer. Who will update you on the statistics and science behind our approach to defeating the Coronavirus."

Chris Whitty gave all the details he needed; he knew that people needed the science behind all of this to really know where things were going. As Doctor Whitty stood at the podium he always imagined in his mind's eye a very timid confused man on his own in a small flat in Rochester. When he spoke Doctor Whitty thought how can I make it less scary and confusing for this man but keep to the facts and truth.

The press waited in their own homes, laptops ready, slightly nervous as their questions rang across the UK and even the world.

"Prime Minister – a question for you, Laura Klunesberg BBC here…. Did we lockdown too late?"

Boris could see Winston at the back of the room. Dressed in his black tie and striped suit, cigar in mouth. Winston smiled and nodded at Boris. This gave him some sort of assurance.

"Who wouldn't be questioning themselves in all of this?" he thought to himself.

Boris had nights where he would talk to himself for hours. "Could we have closed the whole UK many days before? We didn't know where this was going. Maybe, could we, possibly?"

It's like walking through a dark tunnel, with a small torch. You've never been here before. Every few steps a hatch above you opens up and some-one shouts,

"Where are you going, why have you chosen to go that way?"

You and your team are the only ones with the authority to make the decisions and some of the choices you make may be wrong. But these are people's lives and lives matter.

Boris took a deep breath and worked at answering Laura's question.

CHAPTER TWENTY-SIX

Sending the love

It was almost two weeks later that Gary emerged from hospital. He'd broken his left arm and sprained his neck badly, avoided catching the dreaded 'C – Bug' but he had a deep cut on his cheek that needed stitching up. Gary had been very close to not making it that day. The fence had broken his fall and stopped him landing flat on the concrete driveway. Going home was all he'd thought about.

Cards had started arriving at the hospital. In fact so many cards that they had to get help to open them…sadly for Gary the cards couldn't come into his room in case they were infected with Covid. But the staff made sure they took pictures of them and showed him every day.

Dear Gary – we heard about you on the radio this morning. I'm just 12 years old and am finding this lock-up very hard. My Nan has been very poorly. I heard about you saving all those older people and it made me very happy. You are a true hero.

Justin in Salford Manchester.

Dear Gary – some people have been mean during this crazy time. I've helped by taking salmon fishcakes to an old man who lives near me. He said he didn't like salmon fishcakes, so I took them home and took him some cornflakes and a bottle of ginger beer. You have been a legend Gary, very impressed by what you did. Don't do it again though cos you could have died. Stay safe.

Dennis from Cornwall.

Gary – if I was allowed to be near you I'd give you a big kiss and a hug. You are a burning star in the night sky with bells on.

You saved all those people and made the world a better place. I bet the fire was very hot and you felt a little scared. But you won and saved the day!!! Hurray.

                              Alice Dunholm in Scarborough.

Dear Mr Gary – you are the kind of person that this country needs. A fine honest brave man who will always be remembered. Well done and bravo for your kind deed.

                              Denise Van-hoff aged 89 from Devon.

As Gary looked at the pictures of the cards on his phone, he felt a little tear come to his eye. He could see the face of Olga, all sooty and full of fear as the Fire Officer carried her down the ladder. He'd heard that Olga and all of the residents had survived the fire. He couldn't believe that something had been on the radio, something about him.

Just fifty feet away, sat in another bed, on another floor of the hospital, right above him; Gary's mother watched the local TV news.

"Local Man Gary Snark, is making good progress," said the news reporter. "The man who saved the day and many lives at St Bart's care home is going home soon."

Alice Snark had fought a battle with her injuries, battled against a mild case of Covid 19 and had a battle with herself. She had a deep sense that she hadn't been a great help to anyone during this Pandemic. Her little toilet roll scam had made no money to speak of, put her son in a bad place and almost killed her. Not to mention Eric's car. Oh the big dent she'd made as she hit the bonnet. Gary had been unconscious for quite a few days so she hadn't been able to see him. Her Covid diagnosis meant she was just surrounded by nurses that looked like space creatures for days on end. Her plan to get some toilet rolls to the Pygg's had fallen flat – they didn't seem interested in money. Alice breathed a deep sigh. She wasn't even a very good crook.

CHAPTER TWENTY-SEVEN

Good things come to those who wait

The day for Gary to be taken home had arrived.

A very kind hospital driver, a volunteer who was helping to transport people around helped Gary with his case. It would be a very welcome feeling to get back to his own bed. Gary thanked the Hospital staff and walked to the car. As he stepped out of the hospital door bright flashes shot all around him.

He wondered if someone famous was coming out behind him, he turned to look.

A group of photographers and newspaper reporters, trying hard to socially distance while elbowing each other out of the way rushed to him. They were wearing masks and gloves and holding pens and standing almost two meters away from him.

"Gary Gary Gary…tell us what made you be so brave? Why go and rescue all those people? Gary how are you feeling?"

"Gary this Gary That, Gary are you a hero, Gary are you married? Gary, will you tell us your story???"

Gary, slightly shaken stood before them and said

"I've never been very brave. Actually I'm a bit of a coward normally. I wanted to do something good at this time. But I couldn't think of anything that I could do. That morning as I drove to St Bart's I was wondering how I could be a better person. I've been a bit selfish at times recently and felt bad."

Gary could feel the words coming out of his mouth. Almost like a train that he couldn't stop. The reporters looked at him. Gary stopped speaking and looked back. For one moment he was about to tell the local paper, the BBC and ITV that he and his mother had been stealing toilet rolls from St Bart's and selling them. Almost like waking up from a dream he stopped himself.

"But as I turned the corner and saw St Bart's on fire, something just happened. I ran inside and all those lovely people who made me smile every day needed help. I'm not a hero, I'm just a very lucky man that got to help some of my friends." The cameras flashed, shouting and questions carried on as Gary was whisked away down the road.

CHAPTER TWENTY-EIGHT

Change of heart

Alexander Boris de Pfeffel sat looking at his breakfast. Eggs, scrambled not fried, bacon lightly grilled, and two slices of brown bread well buttered and crispy. He liked to have a quiet moment at this time of the day. Time to think and breath. In thirty minutes he would be meeting with his team to carry on the planning of how to get through this. How to save lives and jobs and business and families and hospitals and the list could go on and on.

Winston Churchill had carried on appearing to him for many days and he took great comfort in this. He had a new baby now and his fiancée was doing well, that felt good too. He stood to his feet. Turning to the mirror he stood straight. The mirror was always a good way to start the day. He looked himself straight in the eye and repeated a few lines from Winston's speeches. But the words that always came to mind were the words that Winston spoke directly to Boris. 'Fight hard Boris and you will win'.

Boris felt a wave of strength flow through his body. In the mirror, over his shoulder he caught a glimpse of cigar smoke drifting towards the ceiling. There in the corner chair sat Winston smiling.

On that morning, a little more traffic came down Haddon Street. Alan and Jakub stood facing each other; Alan was wrapping the fishing line in his hands. "Well all this has been very strange indeed," said Alan. "Yes it has Alan."

Jakub looked across at Mrs Snark's house. "Do you think she'll be ok?" said Jakub.

"Well she looked in a bad way when the ambulance took her away. I'm sure the hospital will be taking care of her." Alan sighed a big sigh.

"We never did get to understand the mystery. What was she doing and why come and climb my bedroom wall with a clown mask on?" Jakub had a puzzled look on his face. "Well maybe some thing's go unsolved."

"Nah – the truth will come out," said Alan, "it always does. Maybe we'll just have to wait."

Behind Alan's back, over the road in Tom's house, stood a very nervous Tom. He'd now sold all of the toilet rolls. The secretive person who'd dropped them all off and called him had never appeared. Never asked for the money. Tom had seen the news reports about Gary and his great bravery. What have I done thought Tom; yep I've sold stolen toilet rolls and made a profit off the needs of others. He had no idea about the origin of the rolls, coming from the now burned down St Bart's Probably best that he'd never know. As if guided by some inner wisdom – Tom decided that he was going to use the money to start a campaign to rebuild St Bart's. "I'm going to try to be another hero like Gary," thought Tom.

"Or be another 'hero Tom' like Colonel Tom." He was so filled with energy about his new idea that he threw the window open.

"Hey Jakub and Alan," he shouted. "Fancy being the first to start a fundraising team for St Bart's?" Alan and Jakub were a little startled by Tom's head poking out of the upstairs window. "Sure thing." they shouted back and with that it was agreed.

CHAPTER TWENTY-NINE

The last laugh

The news car, BBC, ITV and other journalists followed Gary's drivers' car as it sped across town. Colin the driver had asked which way Gary wanted to head home. "Well I suppose driving past mum's house on Haddon Street would be a good thing, I can check all is ok."

Colin's white Renault Clio trundled through the streets, still bunting on doors and gates from the VE day celebrations. Just a few people cycling and walking. As they came to the top of Haddon Street more bunting and more people. The cars behind were closer now. The BBC and ITV people hanging out of the car windows. People were coming out of their houses. Some shouting "hurray", people clapping, one man with a trumpet, children waving flags. As Colin's car reached the door of Mrs Snark's house they couldn't go any further. A table had been placed in the middle of the street. On it were some flowers and a pile of cards. People lined the pavements – all exactly socially distanced.

Gary stepped out of the car. Colin stood with him. Behind the table stood Mr. Gibbons, he had a huge smile on his face. "Glad you're on the mend Gary, we were worried about you." Gary walked across to the table, looked at Mr Gibbons and said "You've put out a table across the road, I was just heading home."

"Well it's the only way to stop you and give you a hero's welcome," said Mr Gibbons. "We guessed you'd come and check on mum's house."

The people spread across the doorways, up the street, all started to clap and cheer and shout.

"Well done Gary." "Hurray for Gary, what a guy!" "We love you Gary!" Mr. Gibbons pointed to the flowers and cards…

"All for you, and a well deserved cheque for five hundred pounds to say thank you for saving lives."

Alan, with his very proud parents, Eric and Jane watched on. Tom stood and felt a sense of good flowing in the air. The Pyggs hugged each other. Gary shook his head and stepped forward to take the cheque from the table. He took a huge breath and said

"I couldn't take this Mr. Gibbons. I've not always been the best at my job and sometimes not a very good person. But you've been a great man to work for. I'd like to give something back to you. I'd also like to thank Alan Sheen for being so helpful and calm in calling the emergency services."

He took the cheque and placed it back on the table. "This is for the 'let's rebuild St Bart's home fund'." Tom stepped forward and said "…We started a fundraiser today …that's the second donation and we're gonna make as much money as we can. We're gonna rebuild St Bart's!!!"

The BBC and ITV and radio and newspaper people all spoke into microphones and scribbled notes down and nodded to each other. In just four weeks from then, over a million pounds would be raised to add to insurance money Mr. Gibbons would receive.

St Bart's would become one of the best homes in the country. Gary thanked everyone and climbed back into the car. The people all cheered again.

Back at the hospital Mrs Snark had a choice to make. Oh she'd seen the Scrooge films and also the Grinch and blah blah blah, mend your ways and be nice. "Yuk." she hated all that. Her son was now a hero and a national treasure. "What to do?" she thought. "This Covid 19 is changing the world, it's bringing out the best in people. Making people put other people first. Bah Humbug," she thought.

"I'm Alice Snark, with the teeth of a shark and the bite of a shark and the smile of a shark." She lay back on her bed and laughed and laughed, pulling the sheets over her head she, Alice Snark, carried on laughing. "I will have a better plan next time," she promised herself.

"If the whole world were goody two shoes and sweet as apple pie, well how dull it would be."

She quite imagined herself as an international diamond thief. Using her powers of persuasion to convince older people who have lots of lovely diamonds to part with them for a very good price. Her smile got bigger. "Or maybe I could steal childrens bicycles, sell them to other children …Sounds like hard work…diamonds are a girl's best friend."

A puff of cigar smoke wisped up to the ceiling from the chair in the corner. She had a visitor.

Outside it began to rain and a dark cloud covered the sun.

About the Author

John lives in Derbyshire UK and for the last few years, well until the world changed shape, he spent lots of time in Islamorada in the Florida Keys. Married to Amanda for 36 years, two children Abi and Josh, and blessed with the most joyful grandchildren Aubin & Belle. John's promised himself that he'd write a book one day, well the day has come. You can check out his music and other stuff at johnstampmusic.com

About the Illustrator

Paul's professional background was grounded in the dramatic and creative arts both as a performer and as an educator. Paul is also specifically trained within the psychotherapeutic use of the creative arts as therapy. This is Paul's first adventure into the world of illustrative art. Paul is based in The Woodlands, Texas, where he lives with his wife Marcela and their lovely daughter Emily.

Printed in Great Britain
by Amazon

50267264R00070